The Good Father

Peter Prince is the author of PLAY THINGS, which won the Somerset Maugham Award, and AGENTS OF A FOREIGN POWER. He has also written several plays for television and the award-winning OPPENHEIMER series as well as the screenplay for the film THE HIT directed by Stephen Frears.

He now lives in London, and is working on another novel.

Peter Prince

The Good Father

Pavanne

published by Pan Books

First published 1983 by Jonathan Cape Ltd
Previously published in Pavanne by Pan Books Ltd
This edition published 1986 by Pan Books Ltd,
Cavaye Place, London SW10 9PG
9 8 7 6 5 4 3 2 1

ISBN 0 330 29612 4
Printed and bound in Great Britain by
Cox & Wyman Ltd, Reading

1

The man was sitting on the floor holding a little boy in his arms – and even if, like Hooper, you were standing behind him and could not see his face, you would guess with a degree of certainty, from the way he was cradling the child, from the way his cheek was pressed against the wispy, yellow-white hair, that it was his own little boy he was holding.

This was in October, October '81, at one of Sam and Sally Stein's Sunday brunches in the house at Stockwell they had bought for seven thousand in 1969 and spent another eleven on doing up. Hooper arrived late from Hammersmith, owing to a minor motor-cycle accident en route. He was dusty, limping slightly, his jacket was torn and, though he did not know it, there was blood on his face from a shallow graze under the left eye.

Sam Stein gave him a glass of champagne and orange-juice, looked him over, and asked with an uncertain laugh, 'how's tricks?'

'Fine,' said Hooper.

The accident had happened on Wandsworth Bridge when Hooper had suddenly thrown both hands in the air in a gesture of utter despair. Released from his guidance, the front wheel of the bike had swerved on to the pavement and he had narrowly missed crashing into the 295 bus-stop. He had had several spills in the past couple of months and for similar reasons. Strangely, while they had left his flesh only mildly bruised, the Kawasaki 400, brand-new four months ago, looked as if it had been worked over with sledge-hammers. Last time he had taken it in to the repair shop the chief mechanic had said, tight-lipped, 'They weren't meant to take this sort of punishment, you know.' He had looked as if he wished there was a charity he could report Hooper to.

Sam Stein now pointed out that there was blood on his face, and asked Hooper if he wouldn't like to visit the bathroom to clean up. Hooper declined, and Sam, baffled, hugged him – and then moved on to more rewarding guests. Hooper's position was: if there is blood, let it be seen. Let's find out if they can ignore *that*!

And they could! The room was full of old friends and, incredibly, not one of them made a move towards him. Their glances would settle on him for a moment, and then skitter off again. From one or two there came half-waves and half-smiles and mouthings of 'Hi, Bill!' But nobody made a move. Incredible! There is a casualty over here, he wanted to yell. There is blood. What do I have to do?

Of course, in some part of him, he knew it was not incredible at all. His brain was roaring along and seemed to contain about 140 separate compartments and in *one* of them he knew it was perfectly all right, this neglect. It was justice and age-old common sense. This sadness, which was so involving for him, and enthralling even, was not at all interesting to other people.

Laugh and the world laughs with you,
Weep and you weep alone.

To which, like a library book annotator, Hooper even in the midst of his frenzy wished to say: How true! Good friends would go a long way with you in your grief, and very good friends would go even further. But even the best of friends had to pull away in the end, and by general consent – his own included – Hooper had just gone on for far too long.

It was perfectly fair. It had happened to others. He was not being singled out. There had been Cathy Tremayne a year ago. Nobody could help her, though they had all run themselves ragged trying. Bill and Emmy Hooper had been woken up night after night, two and three o'clock in the morning, to hear her passionate, miserable monologues: Hooper gripping his phone, yawning; Emmy moving dazedly around the kitchen, making tea, before she came to take over from him, and all the while Cathy's desperate voice ploughing on and on. They had done all they could for her. They had had her to dinner; and had had her to stay; they had taken her out; Hooper had fixed up a temporary job for her at his office, for she often said it was the emptiness of her days that made her nights so horrible. It was no good. In the end they had had to give up, pull away. There was no helping her and she had just gone on for too long. All the other friends had understood. They had given up on her weeks before.

Poor Cathy, Hooper thought, as he started to move through the Steins' long, tasteful living-room, the crowd parting very easily before him. She had always said it was England, its coldness and depression and detachment, that was at the root of her trouble. She had claimed that she felt like an alien here every day of her life. But at the end she had proved herself perfectly English by leaving a note in which she had tried to be humorous. It had even included some TV-comical catchphrase like 'Didn't she do well?', though that wasn't it. Poor, poor Cathy, Hooper thought, close to tears – but then his brain rushed on and on and she became only one of all the objects and concepts he was grasping at: the room, the guests, the food, the drink, and blood, sorrow, treachery, and Sam Stein with an arm round Alice Carew, Kenny and Anthea bickering in one corner, Janey Powell holding court in another, and harsh laughter, cigarette smoke, the smell of breakfast, sunlight through the bay windows, and the uncaring friends . . .

Alice was coming towards him! She had broken away from Sam and was actually moving purposefully in Hooper's direction. However – even in the midst of such grief – his heart lifted at the sight! He was not then entirely alone. One, at least, remained to him. *Alice.*

Dear Alice. They went back so far, the two of them. Had had such times together. Had even been lovers once, long ago, '70, '71. At least had gone to bed a couple of times. Maybe in '72. And now, at this most terrible moment, she was proving herself true to their friendship. He was not alone. Not totally alone. He smiled at her as she approached, a broad smile of welcome.

He was certain that it was truly a smile that he was offering – but, whatever it was, Alice, catching it full-on, stopped suddenly in her progress. Stared at him for a few seconds. And then, making a sharp, right-angled turn, scurried away towards the safety of the crowd at the other end of the room. Hooper stared after her, amazed.

In a while, he put his hand up, scraped it across his unshaven chin, felt his mouth, the lips that were still stretched in his welcoming smile. Only his fingers disclosed the truth to him immediately. The teeth were bared, the corners of the mouth dragged down on either side. No smile at all – it had been a grimace, a *snarl* that he had been offering the poor woman. And what must his eyes have been saying to her at the same time?

Oh, you fool, Hooper murmured softly to himself, his hand dropping away from the traitor lips, his feet picking up again their funereal tread across the burnished pine floor. You have shocked, disgusted, frightened away the very last friend you had left in the world. Oh, you fool . . .

He arrived at the Steins' broad mahogany table. It bore the remains of the brunch. Hooper felt not at all hungry, but he refilled his glass preparatory to continuing his slow, heart-breaking tour. The impulses in his teeming brain had now concentrated down into two options. Should he throw his glass at someone? Or something? Valuable. Which would best get him the attention that he absolutely required within the next ten seconds?

It was then that he discovered the man on the floor. Watching him, this stranger of about his own age, bent over his child, holding him in such protecting arms,

Hooper felt the contrast between this image and his own recent behaviour with terrible sharpness. Through his mind as he watched, over and over, and blocking out all the other thoughts, raced the one thought: 'There – *there* is the good father.' And soon it became too much for him and he had to go. Through the crowd. Then out of the room, then out of the house. Into the empty crescent where he could be – as he deserved to be – alone.

He phoned the Steins' house next day from the office to apologise for having left so abruptly.

'It's OK, Bill,' Sally Stein said. 'Nobody noticed.' Sally was notorious for saying whatever popped into her mind, a trait that some people found endearing.

Hooper was at a stage where half the time he found it impossible to talk to anyone, and the other half he was pushing out pent-up confidences to whoever would listen. So now to Sally he blurted out, 'It was that fellow on the floor with his little boy. I couldn't take it, you see.'

'Roger Miles? Yes, it was awful, wasn't it?'

Awful? he wondered. It was to *him,* of course – but surely a charming sight to any innocent bystander, to anyone who had not sinned as he had sinned.

'How do you mean?'

'Didn't you see? It was *so* ghastly.'

All he had seen of the man, this Roger Miles, was his grey wool sweater, the nape of his neck, and the back of his head as he had bowed over his child. What he could not see, what Sally now described, was that the face of Roger Miles, as he had looked down on his son, was not that of the proud, the secure, the contented father, but had been racked with bitter grief.

'He was crying,' Sally reported. 'Buckets. Well, it's really sad for him, of course. But Christ – in the middle of a party!'

'Why? – What?'

'She's gone off. Pushed off. Taken the kid with her. Roger was only having him for the day.'

'Who's gone off?'

'His wife, of course. Do you know her?' Sally wondered. 'Cheryl Langford?'

Hooper didn't.

'Oh, she's great!' Sally enthused. 'We met her at university. Just after your time. Roger was there too, of course, but he wasn't particularly – you know – prominent. It was quite a surprise when they got hitched.' A thought struck Sally then. 'Hang on . . . You know you and Roger ought to get together. Being as you're sort of in the same boat. Although,' she mused, 'it's not quite the same, is it? Because what happened to Roger wasn't – '

'Wasn't his fault,' he finished for her.

'That's right . . . Still, I think you two would have a lot to talk about all the same. Shall I fix it? What about lunch next weekend? Oh, hang on – ' She stopped suddenly. Then: 'Awful thought. What if he starts crying again? I couldn't stand it twice in a row.' There was a pause as Sally thought it over. 'No,' she decided. 'I think it'll be OK. I believe he only gets weepy when Richard's with him.'

'Richard?'

'That's his little boy.'

So it was arranged. Lunch next Sunday. 'But Bill,' Sally warned. 'You've got to be cheerful too. You known it's been very hard to be around you lately. Was that blood on your face yesterday?'

'Yes, it was, I know I've been a drag. I'm trying to change that.'

'Well, you must, you know. Alice thought you looked like death. She's quite worried about you.'

'That's nice of her.'

'Now you're being cynical.'

'I'm sorry,' Hooper mumbled.

'And it's so unlike you. You always used to be such fun. You made us all laugh . . . Sometimes you could be a bit spiteful,' Sally said judiciously. 'But still you were always lively. And witty. And charming . . .' Her voice trailed away, full of regret. 'What's happened to you?'

'What do you *think* has happened?' Hooper cried out tormented.

'But it's been going on so *long* . . . Can't you be friends with Emmy at least?'

'No.'

'Well, I think it's daft,' said Sally frankly. 'I wanted to ask her over yesterday and Sam said we couldn't have both of you together.'

'You should have asked her. I'm sure she'd have stayed to the end. And I believe the boy friend is extremely nice.'

'Oh, Bill!' Sally sighed. 'You know you've only got yourself to blame.'

2

On Saturday morning Hooper went as usual across the river to the flat that he had lived in for nearly a dozen years with his wife and then with their baby too. As was also usual he did not go into the apartment but stood just outside, head bowed, staring at the parquet floor. Emmy had tried for a while to persuade him out of this silence, making little jokes, trying to start conversations. But he had been invulnerable, and she had given up. So in silence now she buckled up Christopher's shoes and zipped up his anorak. And it was only to the little boy that Hooper said anything and that was only a couple of words of greeting. He did not really see Emmy any more. The wall of his anger stood massively between them. He was quite surprised therefore when at one moment the sound of her voice broke through it and further penetrated the furious blankness of his mind.

'What?'

'He's got a cough,' she repeated. 'He should be indoors really.'

He looked at her for the first time that day. She stood before him, her head bowed as his had been. The small, trim person he had known going on fifteen years – half her life, and a good fraction of his own. For a moment he felt bewildered, felt the absurdity of this. This was Emmy, *Emmy* . . . And then, out of the corner of his eye, he saw the closed door of her bedroom. The arena of her treachery. Even now her lover might be in there, warming up the bed for their forthcoming delights, once he had taken the little boy off their hands.

Anger rose before him, higher than ever. 'I can't take him indoors. I've got nowhere to take him.'

'You don't have to live in that hotel, Bill – '

'Evidently I do,' he sneered. 'Since you're living in my home.'

And then, to cut the danger of this turning into a conversation, he held out his hand.

'Come on, Christopher.'

The little boy looked up seriously at his mother, and then came and took his father's hand. The two set off down the hall. Emmy called from the door. 'If his coughing gets bad you can bring him home early. I'm not going anywhere.'

Hooper did not respond.

They spent the first hour on the Common, starting at the playground up near the Windmill pub. Hooper pushed Christopher to and fro on a swing for a while, and then went and sat on a bench while the little boy tried out the slides, starting methodically on the smallest and progressing finally to the very big one, where a notice warned that the structure was prohibited to children under six. Christopher was under six, but Hooper was sure his son could handle it. He went and stationed himself under the steps until the boy had climbed to the top. Then he went round to the foot of the ramp to watch him come slithering down it, giggling and shouting. The excitement made his cough bad though, so he came and sat with his father on the bench. Near by, an Alsatian dog kept jumping back and forth over the low fence that surrounded the playground. It made Christopher laugh out loud to watch it. Hooper touched the little boy's cheek and found it flaming hot.

After a while they walked across the Common to the café near the bandstand. He bought Christopher a packet of crisps, and himself tea in a plastic cup. They sat outside at a table. Hooper blew on his tea to cool it and stared at the bandstand. It was a small, snug structure, ornate and pretty. Victorian or Edwardian, Hooper supposed. Anyway it had lasted. Latterly whoever ran the Common had lavished some care and a little money on it and the metal tracery that supported the dome gleamed with fresh bold coats of green and red and yellow paint. Rasta colours. Hooper, when he had first seen it, had saluted this adornment as a thoughtful attempt to harmonise the old and the new. He should have guessed the new would not put up with it for very long. For some weeks now the bandstand's smart appearance had been marred by the names 'Terry T' and 'Danny T' that had been whitewashed in yard-high letters around its concrete base. Suddenly Hooper felt a stab of enormous hatred towards Terry T and Danny T. Vandals. Oafs. Warmongers against the peace, security, and beauty of the community. It was Terry T and Danny T who roamed the Common in sly, unstoppable, predatory bands, tearing down the paling fences, uprooting the newly-planted trees, hurling bricks and tin cans at the ducks and geese on the ponds. Terry T and Danny T who bullied little children, extorted their few coins of pocket-money. And pursued women with their taunts and threats. And under cover of darkness waxed ambitious and deadly. A few weeks ago, after midnight, a man, perhaps a homosexual, had been found stabbed to death in the undergrowth. Between the hours of dusk and dawn the Common lay empty, desolate and embattled. Terry T and Danny T had made it into the mirror of their own bleak souls. He would like to kill them. No less. To take the youths –they would have to be young certainly, fifteen or sixteen – and stand them against the concrete base of the bandstand they had defiled and . . . and . . .

Images of cracking bones and spurting blood disordered Hooper's vision. He shook his head to clear the red fog from his eyes. He was started and horrified by the fury of his reaction. What was it really? Just a stupid prank. Terry T and Danny T were probably a couple of mischievous nine-year-olds. He held his breath for a moment and felt his anger retreating slowly into himself, washing around inside, dissipating painfully into his gut. When he was almost calm again, he looked at his son who was licking crisp crumbs off his palms. Hooper wondered if he should start up a conversation with him, for they had barely talked today. But he was afraid to. Sooner or later the name of Emmy's lover would come up, and he hated that and was scared he would take it out on the little boy.

In a while they started off towards the far side of the Common. It was a dark, sodden, autumn day and, away from the café, there were very few people about. Halfway to their goal Christopher's shoe came undone. As Hooper stooped to buckle it up again, he saw the Common for the first time as a child might see it. A great, grey, empty priarie stretched forth in every direction. In the distance, all around, ran a metal ring of traffic, grumbling angrily. Then more prairie. Then dark houses. Then the blank and lowering sky. It hardly needed the huge black mongrel that squatted near by, squeezing out foot-long turds, to make the point. It was not much of a world to bring a child into. Hooper wondered if his own would ever forgive him. He looked up to see the little boy smiling down at him, though his nose was streaming and his face was feverishly bright. He stood up and gathered the child into his arms. 'Let's get you indoors.'

He carried him most of the way to the McDonald's at the Junction. En route, he stopped at a newsagent and bought a listings magazine, and while his son dabbled happily with his hamburger, he studied the cinema offerings. There would be nothing round here, he knew. Both the local cinemas had closed within the past year. He looked a little further afield. Streatham, Tooting, Chelsea, Fulham. Nothing. He looked further and further. Kensington, Putney, Peckham, Lewisham, Westbourne Grove. There seemed nothing in the whole gross city he could take his boy to, except things he had already taken him to. In the end he closed the magazine and asked, 'Chris, did you like *Superman Two*?'

'Yes,' said the little boy. He was carefully tying a knot in his milk-shake straw.

'Would you like to see it again?'

'OK', he agreed cheerfully.

They took a taxi to the Streatham ABC, for Hooper was not going to risk his son on the pillion of his bike. Ten minutes after the film began, Christopher fell asleep and didn't wake up until his father nudged him as the closing credits started up. On the way home the boy seemed chirpier after his rest. They sang songs together in the back of the taxi, things Christopher had learned at school:

> Red and yellow and pink and green
> Orange and purple and blue,
> I can sing a rainbow
> Sing a rainbow
> Sing a rainbow too . . .

When Emmy opened the door she smiled with relief.

'He looks *much* better,' she said, hugging the little boy.

Hooper started off down the hall.

'Are you *sure* you wouldn't like to come in for a cup of tea?' she called after him.

'Are you *sure* you wouldn't like to come in for a cup of tea?' he mimicked her voice, her high anxious wistful female voice. He pushed his way through the swing doors of the building and out into the street. It would be another week before he could allow himself to push his way back in. As he rode home his head under the scarlet crash-helmet was aching with all the fury that boiled around inside it. On Lavender Hill the exhaust fell off the Kawasaki. He just left it lying there.

3

At the Steins' home next day Hooper tried hard to remember his promise to Sally to be cheerful, and not make an exhibition of himself. In the morning he had found an open-7-days repair shop and had had a new exhaust fitted to the bike. And he took care that it should be a safe trip over to Stockwell. There would be no blood this time. In the house, when he felt the sadness inside him rising too close to the surface, he ducked his head so that no one should see into his eyes. But this did not happen often. For once he was not entirely absorbed in himself. He was also busy studying the stranger who he had last seen cuddling his son in this house, and who –unbeknown to Hooper – had been crying his heart out.

He did not get much chance to talk to Roger Miles during lunch. They were far from being the only guests. Hooper hadn't expected they would be, for the Steins' get-togethers had a habit of swelling from their conception as first Sally and then Sam thought of people it would be fun to have around and got on the phone to ask them along. There were about twelve or thirteen people round the table, as well as the hosts, and talk was lively and general and fairly deafening at times. Sam was a barrister and several of the people here today were connected with the law in some way. Jane Powell had just quit private practice and now worked for a law centre, and a man called Mark Varda – whom Hooper had not met before – was a barrister in the same chambers as Sam. Paul Mosby had qualified as a barrister too but had never practised, working instead as the legal correspondent of a Sunday newspaper.

Having been so often to Stein parties, Hooper knew how dull legal shop-talk could be. But conversation at this lunch was more generally interesting. Though several months had gone by since the big riots of the early summer, the location of the lunch-party – so near to the heart of the storm in Brixton – naturally turned the minds of the guests in that direction. Jane Powell was still maintaining that a legal amnesty should have been given to all those arrested in the street-fighting. The new man, Mark Varda, opposed her, insisting that if you did that you could hardly then deny a similar amnesty to anyone that got arrested during, say, a National Front riot. On the whole most people seemed to support Varda's view of things, and this moderate attitude was so surprising to Hooper that for a moment he ceased his covert study of Roger Miles and looked round the table at his friends with puzzled eyes, wondering if it was at last the first frostings of middle age he was seeing in their caution.

For it had always been, his circle of friends, strongly libertarian and left-wing in outlook, ever since it had come together in the exciting days of the late 'Sixties. All through the bleak mid- and late- 'Seventies the friends had kept the faith, suffering only the occasional drop-out and backslider. This, Hooper knew, though he kept it to himself, was not entirely to his own liking. He sometimes thought enviously of people outside his circle, and of circles other than his own that had bowed to the temper of the times and had sunk into a restful immobility. But not his own crowd, and it was the women he largely blamed for this. (For a moment Hooper wondered if 'blame' was quite the word he wanted – he found that it would do.) On the whole, he felt, the men in the circle, if given the chance, might well have slithered away from the good fight by now, and got themselves absorbed in hobbies, say, or their careers or exercise or meditation. It was the women they knew that kept them up to the mark.

They were a formidable bunch. Jane and Sally and Alice and Amy and Anthea and Emmy, though she more than the others seemed to be able to switch her commitment on and off. (Although perhaps it was only that Hooper had seen her in many more moods than the others.) They had a degree of magnificence for him, the women. Sometimes their names seemed to ring out to him like a roll-call of heroes or the line-up of a World Cup team. Powell and Stein and Carew and Dunn and Ritchie and Hooper . . . Yes, even his own name, and even Sam's, seemed formidable to him within this galaxy. In the old days, the first days, during the student movement and the Vietnam War protests, it had been the men in the circle who had made most of the running. The upsurge of feminism had changed all that, leaving the men gasping, bewildered, and bruised – for as the nearest to hand they had naturally been the first and easiest targets of the women's rage – and sending the women into apparently permanent overdrive. And it was for these powerful women, at their behest it seemed to him, that after his own initial fire had died away he had kept on turning out for demonstrations, pickets, rallies, conferences – all the while a voice inside him murmuring the beginnings of questions that he did not quite have the nerve to finish. Such as 'What am I – ?' and 'Why am I – ?' and 'What's the bloody point of – ?'

It was not, thought Hooper, that he had really grown any doubts about the basic righteousness and correctness of the cause. (Well, he had . . . one or two . . . but let it alone.) It was just that . . . he was tired. It had been going on so long. It was like being in the Thirty Years War. It was surely time at last for him to come home – to applause? – and hang up his helmet and let somebody else do their share. But no. There was to be no truce. No let-up. No backing down. And all – almost all, Hooper felt – for the fear of looking bad in women's eyes.

Where had it come from, this fear, this guilt, among the men of his circle? Surely from very far back. The hand upraised, soft, powdered face stern, plucked eyebrows of the 'Forties arched in scorn, the lipsticked mouth a disapproving gash . . . Nowhere to hide. No forgiveness. No escape . . .

From these troubling, complicated thoughts, it was a relief for Hooper to turn back to his inspection of Roger Miles. He was sitting on the opposite side of the table, three or four places down. Roger was not, as Hooper realised he had half-expected him to be, actually in tears. He seemed quite cheerful and in control of himself. He was a big man, strong about the shoulders and chest, but with a patient, almost submissive face. ('The willing ox,' Hooper dubbed him to himself.) His fair hair was thinning noticeably – something Hooper was not likely to miss, with his own good head of light-brown hair, in which not one single thread of grey had yet appeared. He, like Hooper, made little contribution to the conversation, eating steadily throughout the meal, except when some particularly lively point was being made, when he would lean his large head to one side and watch the speaker with amused and interested eyes.

Only once was Roger pulled into the discussion. That was during dessert when the conversation had moved on from the legal aspects of the riots to their underlying causes. Mark Varda was poking fun at the general assumption that they were principally due to unemployment. 'These kids don't want jobs,' he smiled, looking round the table. 'At least not the sort of jobs they're equipped to do.' Several guests were grinning involuntarily, in sympathy with his high good humour. 'They can't add two and two together very well,' Mark Varda went on, 'but what they would like to be, you see, is president of IBM or a TV star or John McEnroe or NATO Commander-in-Chief. At the very least they might consider airline pilot or open-heart surgeon. They're living in a world of near-complete fantasy, these kids, I promise you.'

Shockingly in a way, only Jane Powell stuck up for the honour of the group's past. 'Oh what crap!' she cried.

Mark Varda smiled affectionately across the table at her. 'Ah, Janey,' he sighed. 'Still battling after all these years!'

She refused to be charmed. 'What do you know about unemployed kids, Mark?' she demanded. 'You don't know anything about them.'

'None of us does,' somebody said mournfully, and several heads nodded ruefully round the table, although Sam Stein wanted to argue the point.

'I defend them all the time,' he claimed.

'Yes, but that's not the same as *knowing* them,' several voices chimed in.

'Roger should know them,' somebody else said. 'He's a teacher.'

Everyone turned to look at Roger. He smiled apologetically at the ring of faces. 'I only teach juniors,' he said. 'At that agc they're very nice. Very willing . . . ' He stopped.

After a moment Alice Carew said sadly, 'You know, I can remember when we called *ourselves* "the kids".' Conversation then turned down familiar paths as they rehearsed yet again the reasons that had made theirs – in their eyes at least – such a great generation. Old politics. Old loves. Amy Dunn spoke fondly of Bertrand and the barricades of Paris in '68. Sam Stein, for perhaps the hundredth time, related how as a youth in Leeds and into his first year at university he had been a 'red-hot Young Conservative' until – a loving glance at his plump, pretty, smiling wife – 'she took me in hand'. Even Janey Powell, though reluctant at first, was finally nudged and teased into contributing her piece about a boy called Raoul, met while cutting cane in Cuba with the Venceremos Brigade in 1970 – Jane, who of all the circle was the most opposed to its tendency to wallow in the past and who, in her strong, dour fashion, had tried to show by her work at the law centre, in her local Labour party, and as a borough councillor that there were other ways of maintaining the struggle than just reliving the gaudy glories of the past.

For this she had been rewarded behind her back with the nickname of 'Saint Jane' – and invention of Hooper's originally. It had been meant mockingly but, though nobody would dare use it to her face, in time the title had come to denote something of the respect they all felt for her, for her straightness and hard work and refusal to take the easy ways. But even she today relaxed and joined in the delicious tickling of the tribal bones.

And as they listened or as they chipped in with their own anecdotes, the friends grew animated, relaxed, convivial. Tiredness and strain seemed to drop away, and while they talked and listened they leaned eagerly towards each other. Sometimes they reached out and touched one another tenderly, and having touched, they stayed, hands entwined, or resting an arm on another's shoulders. It was like the meeting of old lovers who still wished each other very well. For several here this was literally the case. The late-afternoon sunshine, pouring through the bay windows, bathed the group in a kindly glow and, after a while, it was as if in this light and in this setting and by their words the years and their exhaustions dropped away like irrelevancies and they became for each other just what they had been when they had all first met: young men and women on the verge of life. In truth, none of them here was so very old. Even Paul Mosby, the oldest, was only a year or two past forty. But still . . . to be *really young* – and, as they kept assuring each other, at such a marvellous time to be thus. It was the sweetest feeling, experiencing it again.

Unobtrusively, the Steins all the while kept the party supplied and running. There was wine enough. Fruit. Nuts. The coffee arrived just when everybody wanted it, and the talk and laughter never ceased. 'Why it's like Christmas!' Amy cried out at one point, and people laughed delightedly for that was exactly what it was like.

'A good Christmas though,' somebody added. 'Don't forget there have been some rotten ones.'

And Paul Mosby started up, 'Do you remember that

Christmas when we all got food poisoning?'

There was a chorus of comic groans and shudders.

'The turkey!'

'Vomiting!'

'The runs!'

'It was Kenny's fault. He cooked it.'

'He left the giblets inside. And the bag they came in.'

'Bullshit!'

'Oh, yes, you did!'

Only three guests remained aloof from the fun. Hooper said nothing, though in the past he had usually enjoyed this sort of talk. But recent experience had made him sceptical of the value of ancient friendships, and in this mutinous spirit he found himself reacting quite strongly against the mood of the gathering. At one moment a memory came to him from the era that his friends were now celebrating, and he mulled over it sourly. A rock concert somewhere under a drizzling sky. All around were thousands of spectators, wrapped up in polythene sheets, lying in the mud and filth. Above the grovelling masses, helicopters flew transporting the entertainers, their hangers-on, whores, and dealers to and from the privileged areas. There used to be an old tramp who showed up on these occasions. His name was Godfrey and he had discovered that if he wrapped a colourful scarf round his snarled grey hair and sewed a flower-patch on his rags it entitled him to grope all the hippy girls he could get his hands on. And leech off them for money, food, drink and shelter – it must have seemed like American Express to Godfrey. At one point Hooper had been in the first-aid tent where a young girl was gradually, fearfully, piecing herself together after a disastrous drug debauch. Godfrey had lumbered amiably in and had made straight for her and had begun pawing her breasts and slobbering all over the poor, dazed, crazy face. And nobody had stopped him! Nobody had kicked the old brute out of the tent! Somebody, inevitably, had murmured 'Far out!' The girl had gone into a screaming fit eventually.

Hooper shuddered at the memory, and to help rid himself of it turned again to his study of Roger Miles. He too was taking no part in the conversation, in fact his expression had grown sombre and remote. Watching him, Hooper felt a thrill of recognition and sympathy. At last he believed he was truly looking at another man to whom the worst thing in life had happened.

Finally, though Hooper hardly registered it, Mark Varda too made no contribution, only sitting and watching the others, his swarthy face set in an expression of amused but sincere contempt.

Around four o'clock the guests departed, most of them still wrapped in a warm fug of nostalgia. As their cars started to roar away out of the crescent, Hooper turned to Roger Miles, who was standing next to him on the front doorstep, and asked him if he needed a lift. In his hands he was cluthing his spare crash-helmet. He had bought it months ago with exciting visions of all the new women he would soon be persuading to sit astride his pillion seat. Now he held it out hopefully to Roger Miles.

Roger said it was OK, he had his car with him, thanks.

Hooper nodded. He felt extremely self-conscious. 'The thing is,' he said at last, 'I didn't get a chance really to talk to you and . . . well, Sally says . . . apparently . . . we've got something in common.'

'Yes,' said Roger Miles, looking in his turn awkward and shy. 'Yes, she mentioned it to me too.'

They stood there, looking mostly at each other's shoes. Finally Roger broke into an embarrassed laugh.

'Well, look, you know,' he said. 'I mean, if you're not busy . . . if you want to come back to my house for a cup of coffee?'

'Right,' Hooper agreed swiftly. 'Where do you live?'

'Clapham Common . . . The wrong side.'

'Sorry?'

'It's in a book by Graham Greene,' Roger smiled. 'He has the narrator say something like: "I lived on the south side of the Common. The wrong side".'

'I see.'

There was a pause during which Hooper was aware that his smile was becoming increasingly fixed and stale. This did not augur well, he thought. He was not at all sure what he wanted from Roger Miles, but swapping literary tags wasn't it.

'You'd better follow me,' Roger said at length. And without another word they went to their separate vehicles.

4

Roger Miles lived in a small terraced house on one of the roads that led off Southside. Immediately Hooper got inside the front door he looked keenly around for evidences of the tragedy that had recently happened here. He was quickly rewarded. A child's hobby-horse was standing against the wall, just inside the door. He stared at it, and then at Roger with passionate sympathy.

'Kitchen's through here,' Roger said.

After he had plugged the kettle in, Roger Miles looked around his little kitchen and hummed to himself. It was clear to Hooper that neither of them knew how to begin this encounter. He had no ideas. The humming died away. The silence hung thick and awkward. Until Roger, the braver or more generous, made an attempt.

'Pretty good lunch, wasn't it?'

'Not bad. Did you know many people?'

'Not really. Just the Steins. And Kenny . . . And Alice.'

'Not Amy? Everybody knows Amy.'

'Which was she?'

'Amy Dunn. On my left. Nice lady. Nice to look at. If your taste is Mary Poppins,' Hooper added. (He had used to be known for his malicious quips in the days when he felt safe and in control. Perhaps, he had a sour, darting hope, this was something of a return to form?)

'No. I don't know her.'

Conversation died. Roger went to get cups from the shelf. Hooper found himself staring at where, beside the door, a series of pencil marks had been scored into the white wall, one on top of another. And beside them were written dates: 12/3/79, 1/2/80, 10/5/81 . . . He didn't need to ask what they were there for. He knew they recorded the glorious growth of a child.

'So your wife took your boy away too?'

Hooper looked up. Roger was standing at the sink watching him seriously.

'More or less.'

'It's bloody awful, isn't it?'

'Yes.'

They were silent again, until the kettle started to whistle. As he was heaping out instant coffee into two mugs, Roger asked, 'Did you know Cheryl?'

'Who?'

'My wife.'

'Ah . . . no,' Hooper said. Then, politely, 'I've heard she was interesting.'

'Oh, yes,' smiled Roger affectionately, as he brought the mugs to the table. 'She was. She was definitely that.' He stirred his coffee, still smiling to himself. 'I can still hardly believe she married me.'

'How's that?'

'Well . . . we knew each other slightly at university. But then . . . well, you know, she was quite a star there. And I . . . ' He grinned sheepishly. 'I wasn't a star at all. I think I was quite young then, actually,' he added seriously. 'For my age.'

'But she was a star?'

'That's right . . . Anyway. We met again at a party in '76 and – '

'Got married.'

'Six weeks later.'

'And had a kid.'

'Yes. The first year . . . well, she wanted a baby as soon as possible. She was past thirty, you know . . . '

'And then she went off?'

' . . . Right.'

'Taking the child?'

Roger Miles nodded.

'Any warning?'

'Not really . . . She was just gone one day when I got back from work.'

'You didn't talk about it? About the kid?'

'No. Don't recall that we did.'

You poor sap, Hooper thought. And all you ever were to her was a spunk factory. He studied the unfortunate man opposite with feelings that hovered between contempt and pity.

But Roger Miles unexpectedly had started to giggle. He checked himself when he saw Hooper's puzzled frown. 'Cheryl at university,' he explained. 'She was amazing . . . She got sent down in the end.'

'Why?'

'She put acid in the punch at a St Valentine's Day dance,' Roger chuckled.

'Stupid bitch!' Hooper snapped. Then remembered that he was a guest and that he hardly knew his host. 'Sorry,' he muttered.

Roger nodded understandingly. 'No, I suppose it was pretty bad in hindsight.' Then he chuckled again. 'But it was hilarious at the time. As long as you hadn't drunk any . . . ' He cackled suddenly at some further happy memory. And then sobered up. 'Actually there was quite a row about it. They called the police in. She got put on probation, poor thing.'

Hooper stared at the height marks beside the door. 'You seem very forgiving,' he said.

'What?'

'Well, I think I'd be quite angry if my wife had just walked away with my kid.'

'I thought she had,' said Roger Miles.

Hooper was silent for a time. Then admitted, 'The truth was it was me that left Emmy.'

'Why'd you do that?'

'Because it wasn't good any more . . . ' For a moment he dwelled in the last bad years of his marriage. The stupid adulteries they each had committed. The poverty of their own love-making. The growing fierceness of their arguments. The despairing sense that each was to the other both captor and prisoner . . . 'We used to tell people,' he said slowly, 'that we'd met the right person, both of us, but we'd met them too soon. We were very young when we met,' he explained. 'She certainly was.'

'But she was the right person?'

'I don't know. Perhaps.' Then, 'She fucking wasn't by the end.'

'So you left her.'

'Yup.'

'And the boy.'

In pain Hooper cried out: 'How could I leave my boy?'

'I'm sorry,' Roger murmured after a moment. 'I thought you said . . . '

Hooper could not understand it. He had thought he had covered everything when he made his plans to escape from his old life. And he was not – he thought, he hoped, he begged to be reassured – not a complete fool surely. In his job he was accustomed all the time to dealing with probabilities, contingencies, cause and effect, the scientific computation of the possible elements in a given situation. The contingency that Emmy, once he had roared out of her life astride his new machine, would take up with another man – that had occurred to him, of course. Why shouldn't she? That it would hurt to discover she had someone new, that in his hurt he would come to believe he still wanted her, that she would then in her turn refuse to have him back – all these and many other possibilities he had foreseen before he left, if only in a cloudy disbelieving way. But then how had it happened – monstrously – that in all his plans and strategies and pre-visions he had overlooked one colossal item?

He had overlooked Christopher.

He had overlooked his darling son.

He had let another 'father' in the door.

This thought was so shocking to Hooper, what it said about himself was so disgraceful that – though he knew he had to find out how the disaster could have possibly happened – he could never endure harbouring it for long. So now, in Roger's kitchen, he took refuge from the torment as usual in violent anger, as usual against Emmy:

'The bitch,' he rasped. 'The sly, bloody *bitch* . . . '

But even to himself the accusations on his lips seemed so unconvincing that he became ashamed. He lowered his head wearily. 'She shouldn't have,' he muttered. And then, hopelessly, 'I shouldn't have . . . '

After a moment, Roger said gently, 'I'm really sorry.'

Hooper looked up and saw that the other really did look sorry, his head leaning on one side as he had seen him do before, his eyes mild and troubled. Hooper couldn't help feeling warm towards him. And then he felt ashamed for, though he craved it, he knew he didn't deserve any sympathy. Still it was good to have. It calmed him very much.

'Well,' he said at length, 'it's not so bad as for you, is it? I mean, you're blameless.' He stared at Roger, puzzled. 'And you're not angry.'

'Angry?'

'She stole your son.'

'He's half hers,' Roger Miles demurred.

'And he's half *yours*. My God!'

Roger frowned thoughtfully. 'I hadn't thought of being angry,' he explained. 'Just miserable . . . She lets me see Richard whenever I want to.'

'Big of her!' Hooper snapped. He finished his coffee. He was beginning to feel irritated at Roger Miles's passivity. He thought he might as well go. There was nothing much for him here. He wanted a confederate in his fury, not lessons in patient forbearance and turning the other cheek.

'I can't really ever allow myself to get angry,' Roger said, suddenly, pensively. 'Because of my job. Teaching . . . I feel if I ever let myself get really angry –' He bunched his fingers together and Hooper found himself staring at a pair of truly huge fists. 'I could do a lot of damage,' Roger ended gently.

They looked at each other across the table. Then Roger smiled. 'Want another cup?'

'OK,' said Hooper.

When Hooper finally left, about an hour later, Roger Miles suggested that they got together again soon, each bringing his child along too.

'Do you live around here?' he asked.

'Not any more,' Hooper said. Then added, 'I don't really live anywhere at the moment. I'm staying in a hotel in Hammersmith. Single room. Share kitchen and toilet. Six fifty a night. Easy access to the flyover.'

'Why are you doing that? It sounds gruesome.'

'Yes.' Hooper had a brief grisly vision of his room. 'Yes, it's amazingly bad. I should be looking for somewhere proper, I suppose.'

'Why aren't you?'

Hooper shrugged.

'Sounds to me,' Roger observed, 'as though you've been trying to mortify yourself.' And added with a smile, as Hooper stared at him. 'A hair shirt would have been simpler.'

It was hardly a joke at all, a bit of teacherish banter – but Hooper wasn't expecting it, and he laughed out loud. The first moment of pure merriment, he realised later, that he had enjoyed in months. They fixed a meeting for the following Sunday. And riding back to Hammersmith, Hooper did feel that a chink of light at last had shown itself in the universal blackness that surrounded him – a feeling that did not linger, however, much beyond his first thirty seconds inside the Sandringham Hotel.

After half an hour in his room, Hooper knew he could not stand to be alone this night, and he seized his motorcycle things and went outside. In his mind he flipped through the tally of the people he knew. He rejected them all. Rather, he rejected himself on their behalf. They had seen enough of him, all of them. Last time he had taken his cares and woes round to Kenny Herbert's place, Anthea had refused to let him in the door. 'He's not here,' she'd said. But he had been. Hooper had spotted Kenny peeping nervously out at him from an upstairs window. He could not face another such experience. He was not sure that there was any door in London that would open to him tonight, certainly none that would open gladly.

Nine o'clock came, then nine-thirty, then ten o'clock came and found Hooper still sitting on the steps outside the Sandringham, his battered helmet in his lap, wondering what to do next.

5

He spent a good part of the next few Saturdays in the company of Roger Miles. The little boys got on well together. Richard at four-and-a-half was a few months older than Christopher, but he was a gentle child, mild like his father, and didn't seem to mind particularly following the lead of the more adventurous Christoper. Some of the best times they all had were out on the Common, and Hooper was amazed to see how that patch of land, so often empty and forbidding when it was just him and Christopher out there, seemed mysteriously to become populated and full of incident now there were four of them. The little boys ran ahead of their fathers, flushing out rabbits and squirrels from the thickets, or gawking at the anglers at the Mount Pond or the teams of Rastafarian soccer-players or the old men playing chess in the huts by the café or the lone young men and women out on the grass, facing the sun, practising T'ai Chi. Behind them came the two men, often in contented silence, but even more often deep in conversation.

They found out they had both been born in the southern London suburbs and had grown up five miles apart. Hooper was a couple of years the older and had been married much longer. Roger seemed to enjoy his job more but – though it appeared to embarrass him to reveal it – Hooper, as a marketing manager at Overton's, the large but not distinguished publishing house, earned over twice Roger's salary.

'Would I have read anything you've marketed?'

'*Diana – Our Princess of Hearts?*'

'No, don't think so.'

'Or *Blades* – the story of ice-skating in thirty-six weekly issues, complete with set of leather-like binders?'

'No. Missed that one too.'

'It's mostly that sort of thing,' Hooper said. 'One-offs, part-works, souvenirs . . . rubbish really.'

'How did you get into it?'

'Not sure . . . Well, after the wedding, me and Emmy travelled for ages. When we got back to London I wanted a job in journalism. But nothing doing . . . So after about six months I took this job at Overton's in the marketing department. And stayed. I thought I'd switch over to Editorial when something came up. But I didn't.'

'Why not?'

'Don't know . . . Well, the way they treat people in Editorial is a scandal. They're all young kids from university. They get hired for a particular project. Short contracts. Rotten salaries. The moment their project's finished they get booted out. I thought: who needs this? I'm better off where I am . . . '

(But Hooper was aware he was not being entirely frank in this account. In fact, in those days he had no real burning desire to be a journalist or an editor. What he wanted above all was to be what he though of as a 'real writer'. He took the job mainly to pay the rent while he worked nights and weekends at his writing. Within four years he had six unfinished novels and four unfinished play-scripts stored in a tea-chest in his and Emmy's bedroom. It came to him gradually as he started on his seventh novel that he was no longer working at Overton's to support his writing, but that he was writing to justify to himself his staying at Overton's. When he realised this he stopped writing. By now he had received several promotions at work and pay-rises which lessened the pain of his defeat and reconciled him to staying on. No one else except Emmy knew about his efforts to be a real writer, or of his failure. He hardly ever thought about that now. He certainly didn't want to talk about it. He had never been able to throw away the piles of manuscript in the tea-chest though.)

'So I stayed in Marketing,' Hooper said. 'And stayed at Overton's. Like an idiot . . . No, it's not so bad,' he relented. 'The work's sort of interesting . . . sometimes. It's a very sales-oriented firm so a lot of projects get cooked up in my department or in Advertising. So I have a kind of editorial function . . . And I like my office. And I've got friends. I've got Creighton.'

'Who?'

'Creighton Phillips. My pal. He's in Advertising. We have a lot of laughs together.' Hooper stopped. He could not just now remember the last time he had had a laugh with Creighton Phillips. Or had even talked to him. The past few months in the office were a complete blank in his mind. 'Creighton's a sort of funny drunk,' he began slowly. And then stopped again, confused. When *was* the last time he had talked with Creighton Phillips? And what had they talked about?

Back in the house, Roger seemed thoughtful as he made the tea.

Finally he said, 'You know, Bill, with the sort of money you're making you could afford somewhere quite nice to live.'

Hooper said nothing.

'Are you giving Emmy a lot?'

Hooper shook his head. 'The rent on her flat's hardly anything. And she makes money. She edits maths books and papers and things at home . . . I put in a hundred a month towards Christopher's food and so on.'

Roger look surprised. 'That's less than I give Cheryl.'

Hooper stared. 'You give her *money*?'

He nodded. 'Well . . . she never was much good at earning. When I met her again she'd been living on social security for years. I mean, she was pretty destitute.'

'How sad!' Hooper fumed. 'How much are you giving her?'

'About two hundred and fifty a month. I can't afford any more.'

Hooper shook his head in wonderment. 'You are paying this woman,' he said slowly, 'two hundred and fifty quid a month for the privilege of having her steal your kid away from you?'

In silence Roger Miles placed the teapot on the kitchen table. He sat down. Hooper started to say something. Roger looked up.

'Don't ever say that again, Bill,' he stated. 'I really don't want to hear anything like that ever again.'

Hooper stared across the table. Roger's eyes were grave. His powerful shoulders hunched tensely towards Hooper. 'If you're going to say those kinds of things,' he said, 'perhaps you shouldn't come round here any more.'

The thought of having Roger's home snatched away from him, of Christopher and himself out on their own again in the unfriendly world, scared Hooper considerably. And from that day he tried to hold his peace on the subject of Roger's absent wife and her cruel and arbitrary ways – though it did not mean that he began to think any better of her.

News of his and Roger's growing friendship got round Hooper's old circle. Sally rang him one morning at the office.

'I'm really glad!' she cried.
'Yes, it's nice for the boys.'
'Go on,' chaffed Sally. 'It's nice for you too. Somebody to talk things over with. Maybe you won't be such a misery any more.'
I hope not, Sally. I'm sorry I was such a trial.'
'Never mind. Now you can be your old self again.'
Hooper waited for her to get off the line.
'Well,' she said coyly. 'Don't I deserve a few thanks?'
'Sorry?'
'It was me that did it, remember? Brought you two together.'
'Oh. Right . . . Thank you, Sally.'
'My pleasure!' cried Sally Stein.

6

He reported this conversation to Roger Miles next Saturday out on the Common. 'They piss me off,' he concluded.
'Who does?'
'Women. The women we know. Sally went on at me for half an hour. Friends and friendships. Relationships. Relating. Inter-relating . . . God almighty!'
'Well, they're good at it,' Roger said gravely. 'Women are very good. They've always got this network of pals, and they're always there if things go wrong. They put a lot of energy into it. And I think they're right.'
'I don't care,' Hooper grunted. 'They still piss me off.'
He was in a rage today. He had taken very seriously the warning to keep his mouth shut about his friend's wife. But this Saturday he could not help himself. Roger was understanding, however. For he had heard – as Hooper had winced to hear – little Christopher that morning again

refer to Emmy's lover as 'my other daddy'.

'My other daddy!' Hooper grated. 'And soon the bastard'll be just "daddy" to him. And I'll be – what? "Uncle Bill"?'

'I wouldn't worry about it,' said Roger gently.

'*Why* not? The other sod sees him all week long. I only get him on Saturday. What chance have I got?' Hooper wanted desperately to cry, or hit somebody.

'Look at it this way – ' Roger began.

'Oh, what the fuck do *you* know?'

They collected the boys and started to move them towards the playground. Along the way, they passed a heap of splintered wood that had once been a park bench, sure evidence of the recent passage of Terry T and Danny T. Roger plodded along silently, rebuked. Hooper knew it was unfair of him to lash out at his friend. But he didn't know what else to do with his pain. Hit Christopher?

'How are you going to feel when it happens to you?' he demanded. 'And it will,' he added with aimless malice.

'I don't think so,' said Roger quietly.

'Why not? She could move in with another bloke, any time she wants to. As easy as that.'

'No. It's not likely.' Roger hesitated. Then, tentatively: 'You see, Cheryl's gone to live with a woman.'

The two little boys had run ahead, vying with each other to be first to the swings. Christopher was already well ahead. Hooper gazed at his friend as they walked along. He cleared his throat.

'Live with?'

'Mm.'

'Well, when you say "live with",' Hooper started cautiously, 'do you mean – '

'Well, I mean . . . every way there is.'

'She's gone gay?'

Roger grinned suddenly, shyly. 'Yes, that's what I mean.'

They positioned themselves behind their sons who wriggled and shouted on the swings. Hooper, his mind buzzing at this revelation, started to push his little boy. He judged the children were making too much noise to be able to overhear him, and he said, 'Are you sure?'

'The woman she's gone to live with – she's gay.'

'But that's not proof,' Hooper argued.

'They sleep in the same bed.'

'How do you know?' asked Hooper after a moment.

'Richard told me.'

He had pushed too hard. Christopher rose high into the air, shrieking with excitement. For a horrible moment, at the top of his ascent, he wobbled in his seat and cried out in fear. Hooper caught him as he swung back to land, slowed him down. The little boy yelled for more of the same. But his father, sobered, kept him low and steady.

'Is this something new for her?' he enquired, after a while. And then, immediately, 'Listen, it's no business of mine, if you – '

Roger shook his head. 'No, it's not new.'

'While you were married?' Hooper persisted.

The other nodded. 'She'd have the odd night out. I didn't mind,' he said. 'I liked Cheryl the way she was. And this was one of the ways she was. If it had been another man I might have minded, but . . . '

Hooper nodded understandingly. He has used to despise such clichés, but had become quite interested in them lately. There seemed to be a lot of truth lurking about in them.

Fools rush in where angels fear to tread.

Look before you leap.

Out of the frying-pan, into the fire.

Yes, there seemed to be a world of common sense that he had been overlooking for years.

'Has she always been like this?' he asked.

'Since I met her again. And before that . . . well, I think theoretically long before that.'

'Theoretically?'

The boys were tired of being swung. They wanted to come down, they wanted to go home. Holding Richard in his arms, Roger glanced across at Hooper. His eyes were twinkling, he started to gin. 'I think I'll show you something, Bill,' he said. 'It might give you a laugh.'

'What is it?'

'Um – you'll see!'

He grinned again. He seemed quite excited. Hooper could see his point. It was his friend's chance to show off new sides to his past, to show it had not been all dull plodding back there. Other things had been going on, sophisticated stuff. But Hooper was not altogether pleased to hear this. He had got accustomed to thinking of Roger as a plodder. There had been safety in the idea of such a stolid, stable friend. He felt the ground shift a little beneath his feet.

It was the second time this week he had heard something unexpected about Roger. He had been talking with Sam Stein when Roger's name had come up, and Sam had told him how at a party a few years back he had seen Roger, in a quiet corner, twisting his girl friend's arm.

'Who, Cheryl?'

'No, the one he had before her. She really squealed,' Sam remembered.

'But why would he do that?' Hooper said, amazed.

'Don't know. She was being the life and soul of the party. Perhaps she got on his nerves. He stopped when he saw me looking . . . Christ,' grunted Sam, when he saw that Hooper was still looking astonished. 'I've done some things like that myself. Haven't you?'

'Home?' said Roger.

Hooper nodded thoughtfully.

7

It was a small cyclostyled magazine, crumpled and dusty, issued, Hooper learned from the title page, by the Crouch End Women's Collective in March 1971. Inside was a collection of stories, poems, and articles, including a contribution by Cheryl Langford entitled 'The Way Forward'.

Roger had brought it down from an upstairs room. Hooper had waited in the kitchen, leaning back in a chair, looking out through the glass door. Keen winds were tearing the last leaves from the chestnut tree at the bottom of Roger Miles's garden. Inside, it was warm. They had bought scones for tea, and his stomach was rumbling in anticipation. He was certainly interested in whatever it was that Roger had gone to fetch, but . . . hot scones with runny butter. Strawberry jam. He yawned comfortably.

The little pamphlet landed on the table beside him. He looked up to see Roger grinning at him, that disturbing grin. 'I knew it was lying around somewhere,' he said. 'Read it. It'll take you back.'

Cheryl's article began by recalling the late-'Sixties shooting of Andy Warhol by Valerie Solanas of the Society for Cutting-Up Men. Solanas's deed was to be commended, she wrote, for 'showing the way to cut the Gorgon's knot . . . ' Hooper looked up at this point.

'It gets better,' Roger giggled.

Cheryl called in her opening paragraphs for a virtual holocaust against the male sex. The quasi-innocent would fall along with the wholly guilty, but men had only themselves to blame for that. 'We are raped indiscriminately,' she wrote. 'We are battered, beaten and murdered indiscriminately. Why then should we not retaliate indiscriminately?' The words washed over Hooper as he read, like smoke from distant fighting. They agitated him tremendously. They took him back, as Roger had promised. For he had listened to this for years, applauded it, in other causes used it himself, this elephant-gun of rage and rhetoric. 'No longer the cowering female victim in the alleyway,' Cheryl Langford vowed, 'but the female sniper on the rooftop – that will be the characteristic image of the new age that is dawning.'

Roger laughed out loud as he watched Hooper scanning these phrases. 'Tremendous, isn't it?' he glowed.

Hooper pressed on grimly into the body of the article. After a brief survey of recent genetic research which, it was claimed, had uncovered the inherent structural weakness of the male-producing Y chromosome, she concluded with what might have been bitter humour, 'So we see that from inception the male of the species is a flawed, corrupted being. Indeed, in a strict biological sense, it may be doubted – as many of us have instinctvely doubted – whether he can be properly termed a true human being at all.' Consequently – and Hooper in distress found himself fascinated in old familiar ways by the relentlessness of radical logic – consequently it was advisable that as few as possible of these botched specimens should be brought into the world. 'Feminists will support efforts to extend pre-sexing of foetuses to the earliest possible moment. In this way those of us who still choose to assume the burden of motherhood will at least be spared, by a swift, safe, and early abortion, the indignity and danger of carrying a male infant to full term.' A few male infants would have to be allowed to see the light of day in the foreseeable future for the sake of the propagation of the species. But careful deployment of sperm resources would enable their numbers to be kept to a manageable handful. There would be no loss in emotional terms. Heterosexuality had had five hundred thousand years to prove itself. It was past time for women to wake up from this weary, fruitless dream. 'The Way Forward' was pointed out by the lesbian woman. 'She stands there', Cheryl Langford triumphantly concluded, 'proud, free, independent, inviting. In her arms we will find what was never to be found in the arms of our oppressors: dignity, peace of mind, love without fear. We should gladly embrace her and her splendid gifts!'

'Well, I thought you'd find it quite amusing,' Roger Miles complained when Hooper continued to stare grimly into space some long time after laying the pamphlet aside.

'Amusing!'

'It's a period piece,' Roger argued. 'An antique . . . Cheryl and me used to have great laughs at it.'

'At *what?*'

'Well . . . ' Roger picked up the magazine and scanned it. ' "The female sniper on the rooftop" – that's rather good, isn't it?' He looked up hopefully, but Hooper was still not smiling. 'You take it much too seriously,' Roger grumbled.

'It was meant to be taken seriously, wasn't it? I do it that honour. I don't *patronise* it.'

'Oh balls!' Roger was uncharacteristically snappy, downcast that the joke had fallen so flat. And *hurt* too, Hooper suddenly saw. The poor besotted man was actually hurt that his friend hadn't been charmed by his wife's rampage. He was turning the pages moodily. 'I don't see why you're so excited.'

'Because it's bloody dangerous stuff.'

'Oh come on!' scoffed Roger. 'Look at it.' He waved the magazine at Hooper's face. 'It's a tiny little thing. How many people could ever have read it? Hundred? Two hundred? It's pitiful.'

'That's not the point,' snapped Hooper, though his anger in fact wobbled for a moment. It was in a way pitiful, a windy tirade in an unread rag . . . But to hell with pity, he thought. No one pitied *him*. Rightly. Pity was for the weak. Weak to give, weak to get. 'Not the point at all,' he cried, feeling stronger as he raged. 'She says men aren't human!'

'She's not talking about *you*.'

'I'm a man, aren't I?'

Roger shook his head. 'You take things far too personally, Bill.'

Hooper stared mutinously ahead. 'Jane Powell told me

that once,' he said at last. 'You remember Janey? At the Steins' that lunch?'

'The lawyer?'

'One of them,' Hooper nodded. 'It was years ago. I was driving her and Emmy to a demonstration, something or other. Christopher was in the car. He was just a baby then, new-born – ' He was lost for a moment. He could see so clearly the drab-green carry-cot sat sideways on the little Fiat's back seat. A square of yellow blanket sticking out of the cot, the back of Christopher's head, for he always lay on his stomach . . . 'Anyway – Janey was wearing a T-shirt which said, right across the front: "All men are rapists". I asked her about it,' said Hooper. 'Did it mean: All men are potentially rapists? Because they've got pricks? Like: All women are murderers? Because they could hit me on the head with a hammer if they chose to? No, she said. It means what it says. All men *are* rapists. Just that . . . Well, I got very angry. I mean, if that was the case – Well, they certainly wouldn't want to be driven around by a rapist, would they? So I stopped the car,' he reported with gloomy guilt. 'And made them walk. It was only about two hundred yards now . . . And Jane looked at me as she was getting out – great scorn – and she said – '

'You take things far too personally?'

'Right . . . actually I minded most for Christopher. Who's going to be a man one day. Always providing – ' Hooper reached out and flicked the magazine that Roger held – 'a female sniper doesn't get him first.'

After a moment, Hooper said, 'That's not true. I minded most for me. Janey was my friend. It hurt me.'

And Roger said gently, 'But they were right.'

'Who were?'

'The women. To be so angry.'

'I expect they were.' Hooper felt suddenly tired. 'I frankly don't care any more. I used to care. I used to sit and argue for feminism for hours.' He laughed harshly. 'I used to argue for feminism against *women*. I was such a good boy, you know? . . . It's true!' he cried, for he thought he saw a sceptical glint in his friend's eyes. 'I admired them so much . . .' And it was true. He *had* admired the women, his friends. Not far short of idolatry. From the sidelines, of course, but that was where they had wanted him to be. He had applauded their battles. He had believed in what they were fighting for. Did still believe in it. Only a fool, he thought, would not recognise the validity of their claims. Almost all of them. But above all he admired the sheer grandeur of their attempt to impose themselves on history, to try to turn the thing around. That was magnificent, he thought, that was immense . . .

All these things Hooper felt. And yet when he spoke again, to his distress it was only to dredge up some more foul water from the apparently bottomless well of his anger and bitterness. 'Emmy's group used to meet in our flat,' he reported. 'I used to serve them wine at half-time. I was out in the kitchen pouring plonk, they were in the living-room telling her what an idiot she was to be married to me, to be faithful. Why didn't she wake up? She had nothing to lose but her shackles . . . That was quite all right with me,' he said honestly. 'I wanted to be correct too. So we both went out and fucked everything in sight. And the marriage went down the drain . . . '

He remembered that when he had gone into the living-room he was always greeted by a chorus of hoarse laughter and good-natured (?) insults. 'Enter the villain!' one of them had shouted out once when he had stuck his nose shyly round the door, to be followed shortly by his bashful, ingratiating grin and his trayful of Spanish red. Intolerable! he frowned now, to think of it. Yet he remembered he had rather enjoyed playing the clownish goat to those rowdy, gutsy women, stooping low before each one so she could, almost without stretching, help herself to a glass. It had positively excited him, in fact. Sometimes as he had buttled away diligently amongst them, they had light-heartedly jostled and pinched him. An overflow of high spirits. He understood. He saw again the ring of female faces, bright-coloured and lively from the vital conversations they had been having just out of his earshot. Himself in the middle, the dimpling focus of their attention, for a little while, before they got back down to serious business. A couple of times at least, as he had bent over to offer wine, another woman sitting behind him had seized the opportunity to kick him playfully in the rear. They were not by any means painful kicks. Almost love-pats. And in fact, right now, Hooper couldn't help wriggling quite pleasantly at the memory of them . . .

Then he frowned again, disgusted with himself. Was it just that he was a hopeless, foolish masochist where women were concerned? Was that all it was? It was very flattering, of course, to see himself as having been a spectator – attentive, mostly silent, deeply-moved – at a great historical development. But what if, after all, he had only been a sort of willing trophy, dragged along, squealing excitedly, behind the victory train? A ridiculous, capering attendant to a mob of disordered, power-hungry harridans? What then? And all of them caught up in an entirely marginal charade. Fringe actors in a fringe drama. How did that look?

No. (By now Hooper was no longer aware of where he was. No longer aware either that he had company. He was locked up entirely in his own thoughts.) No. He shook his head violently. It was not like that. It had not been, was not now any kind of marginal drama. And nor were the actresses marginal. Hooper, though, was another matter . . . But what other options did I have? he thought, pitying himself greatly. Except to play the fool. Or the villain. Or the spectator. What other roles were on offer to him, seriously speaking?

One night, highly embarrassed, argued into it by Jane Powell, Hooper had visited a men's group. Held in a house just off the Caledonian Road. He had a rotten time there. Jane had questioned him closely about it the following day.

'What went wrong?'

'Well . . .'

'Didn't you like them?'

'They seemed extremely nice . . . Very depressed though. And the house was bloody cold . . . '

Jane, after she had heard his dismal account, had studied him very carefully. Her conclusion was that Hooper was afraid of confronting his own sadness.

'But why do I *have* to confront my own sadness?' he had argued. Wishing to add, life's bad enough as it is. '*Your* group doesn't seem to do a lot of that?'

'How do you know? And you're wrong. Of course we do.'

But Hooper remembered well how in the kitchen he could hear, though not in detail, the noisy, bracing uproar of the women's group. No sadness he could discern there. Shouts of laughter came from the living-room, and, often, violent, spine-chilling cries of rage and pain. And all the time the active, eager female hub-bub – it never stopped from the moment they bounced in through the front door to the last fond, exuberant goodbyes at midnight. This was what Hooper wanted. To be where the action was.

'And besides,' Jane added crossly, 'we have other jobs to do.'

And I have to confront my sadness, Hooper had thought sourly. One man at the group had spent the whole evening weeping intermittently. Hooper's neighbour had informed him, *sotto voce*, that this sorrowing was because the fellow had just lost access to his little daughter.

'Why?' Hooper had whispered.

'Because he's been behaving very badly.' Hooper remembered this circumstance now with a pang. Wine was served at this gathering too but not, of course, by any hapless fall-gal equivalent of Hooper. The bottles were just opened and sent round the melancholy little circle. The chance to plant a foot gaily on a female bum was not to be part of this evening's entertainment. It would have been obnoxious, appalling to have even mentioned it here. Even dangerous. And yet, Hooper supposed, if the women had ever got around to considering the humiliation they had dealt out to *him* (and to which he had coyly submitted), they would have seen it no doubt as progressive, exploratory, a refreshing exercise in role-reversal. Hooper understood all this. He agreed with it. And it still rankled. A year or two back he had brought it up in conversation with Alice Carew. She had been amazed, dismayed.

'You can't still be angry about that, Bill!'

'Well . . . I am.'

'But it was just high spirits. In a certain, particular time.'

'I know. All the same . . . '

'Oh, *Bill* . . . I remember those meetings. I probably gave you a kick. You were playing at being the buxom serving-wench. We thought you were so sweet, so witty . . . You were one of the few men we thought we could relax with, have fun with. And not take offence.'

'I know. I understand. It's nothing. It's completely trivial. I don't know why I brought it up.'

But yet he thought: in the name of progress, I got kicked in the bum. As a metaphor it had lived healthily in his brain ever since.

'They would probably have happened anyway,' Roger Miles said suddenly.

Hooper looked up, startled to be reminded of his companion.

'What would have?'

'Emmy's affairs. Your affairs.'

'Maybe,' said Hooper eventually. 'I suppose so. I don't know . . . All I do know – ' Hooper stopped. Suddenly depressed, sick and tired with what he was saying. But Roger was waiting expectantly and he felt obliged to heave up one last sour sputter. 'All I know is: where's it all got me? I'm lonely. I'm miserable all the time. I've lost my home and I'm losing my kid. What a dope!'

Jane had urged him to give the men's group one more try. 'Perhaps you just hit a bad night,' she'd said.

'It's possible. This man I met there told me they often have a lot of fun . . . All right. I'll try it again.' But he hadn't. He couldn't bear to. So much depression in one small icy room. Nevertheless, when his friend and colleague Creighton Phillips, to whom he confided some details of his visit, had started to make fun of the men of the group and belittle them, Hooper had got very angry. In fact, they had had a quite serious argument. For Hooper honoured the men's attempt, even if he could not be a part of it.

Fat lot of good that did anyone, Hooper thought.

They sat in silence in the fading light. Occasionally they could hear muffled thuds and shrieks of laughter from the boys playing up in Richard's room.

Suddenly, darkly, Hooper said, 'British movies.'

'What?'

'I'm trying to work out why it all hit me so hard back then . . . See, I never felt very good about being male in the first place. Well, an all-boys' school – ninety-five per cent of them were such *turds* . . . Including me,' he added honestly. 'And I didn't like what I could see ahead of me either.'

'What British movies?'

'In the 'Fifties. Don't you remember? The men in those films . . . ' When he was little, nine, ten, younger – Christopher's age. 'They were always in baggy uniforms, and they looked so hideous . . . ' As he spoke, Hooper couldn't help thinking that if this was any kind of an explanation, it was a very partial one. Still he had started on it, he might as well plough on, it might lead somewhere. 'Don't you remember? They were always shouting at each other . . . '

The Catford Eros, the Lewisham Rex, the Gaumont Bromley – picture-houses, long-dead now, where little Hooper had crouched in the ninepennies, staring up at the huge screen images. 'Bloody Jack Hawkins – he was always in them, torpedoing somebody or other . . . '

For a moment, as he thought of Jack Hawkins, Hooper stopped, confused. He had a sudden memory of the actor in his last appearances, after cancer had attacked his throat, working gamely on, using some voice production method which allowed him to speak in a series of aspirated gulps. Very brave. It had been harrowing to watch him – though this hadn't stopped Hooper imitating Hawkins and his handicap for laughs at several parties . . . But it reminded him of his own father who had died a few years after Jack Hawkins, not from cancer, from strokes and heart attacks. His father had always seemed to him a cold, remote man, sporadically very angry. When he was a young man he had been a golf professional and had won a few tournaments in the 'Thirties. After the war he had failed to re-establish himself as a player. He had gone to work at a club near Chislehurst, a haven for social golfers, businessmen, their wives, colleagues and pesty children. He had ended up managing the place. It was his function to be nice to these people.

It was understood in the family that he loathed the job, it had all been waste, sacrifice. He spent most of his evenings at the club. In his teenage years Hooper would often come back to the house late after a night out and find his father there just back from the club. In the silent house his father would move around him coldly drunk, he would move around his father coldly sober. It had been as though if either of them were to speak it would be to say something unforgivable. And after Hooper left home, they had still not been friends. They had not been friends ever. But after the first strokes had weakened him, his father had shown much sweetness, courage. He had seemed to want his son to be near him . . . it was confusing.

His father's life had overlapped Christopher's by a few months. When they had first shown him the baby he had wanted to hold it. Emmy would not let him for fear that in his weakness he might drop it. Hooper had agreed with her. But it had been a terrible thing to have done to his father, and he had not then known that Emmy could be so ruthless.

'Jack Hawkins?' prompted Roger, smiling.

'Yes, *him*.' Hooper banished all distracting memories, warmed again to his theme. 'And all those other British buggers . . . having fantastic times in prisoner-of-war camps, bullying each other, being cheeky to the Germans . . . And I thought to myself, even then, I thought: have I got to grow up to be *that*?'

But it wasn't the truth, he remembered sickly, not the whole truth. He had feared, rejected, loathed all those great English boobies up on the screen. Certainly. But there had been something else too, seeping into the little boy's soul as he crouched in the front row of the Eros. The lone grey shapes moving across the dark Atlantic. The sea-wolves! Duffel-coated figures up on the bridge. Steely eyes gazing out on the treacherous deep. 'Up periscope!' 'Drop depth-charges!' Magnificent! In *The Cruel Sea* Hawkins had depth-charged a group of British survivors as they bobbed around in the water. How the poor men had cheered as they saw him bearing down on them, apparently racing to their rescue! When the dreadful deed had been done, one of his sailors had yelled out 'Murderer!' at him. A sentimental, working-class voice. But Hawkins had had to do it, of course, for he had believed a U-boat was lurking down there, underneath the doomed men. Magnificent. Appalling. Could the boy Hooper ever rise to such monstrous virile levels? It seemed doubtful.

'Freaks,' muttered Hooper in the kitchen, thirty years after. 'And then the women starting it. What vile beasts we all were. Sick. Dangerous. Inhuman . . . I tell you I felt like a freak back then, a disgusting accident!'

At length Roger stood up. He glanced at the magazine in his hand, then at Hooper. 'If this bothered you,' he said, 'I'm sorry.'

'No,' said Hooper. He dredged up a smile from somewhere. 'No, you're right. It's all years ago. It's pretty funny, I guess.'

He didn't really believe that. But nor did he want, even with Roger, to appear to be nursing a sterile grudge that belonged to another time, another age practically. The women had had the right to be angry, as Roger had said. And everybody had calmed down a lot since then . . . Probably even Cheryl Langford had calmed down.

He asked Roger if this was the case.

'Cheryl?' said Roger, looking up from the magazine. He shook his head. 'Don't think she's interested at all these days. She's got very involved in self-expression through dance and movement lately. Goes to classes in Covent Garden.'

There. Harmless. Classes in Covent Garden. Everybody else had moved on, and he must too. It was a time for reconciliation, healing, a new understanding between the sexes based on mutual respect and consideration. He had read about this.

Besides, who could tell? The world was getting a more dangerous place every day. The old male specialities – aggression, brutality, going berserk – might even come back into style soon! Thus Hooper tried to put a gloss of humour over the problem. Actually, he thought, he wouldn't at all mind going berserk.

He watched Roger who was again caught up in his wife's article, smiling with affection and admiration as he read. Hooper very well understood this, and he smiled himself, genuinely, in sympathy. They had been superb when they were young, the women they had known. You would not find so much passion and attack roaming around free in these days. (Thank God, he thought to himself quietly.) In many respects they had been lucky to have known them.

He stared out at the garden. It was nearly dark. He should take Christopher home soon. He remembered with a pang of disappointment that they hadn't touched the scones yet, and it was probably too late for them now. Now when he looked again at his friend it was with irritation. They would have been much better employed stuffing themselves, he thought, rather than digging around in these sad, old, irrelevant memories.

8

Finally, Hooper met her. He was at Roger's house on a Tuesday evening early in December. As well as their Saturdays, Hooper had taken to dropping in after work one or two days a week. The two would have supper together, chat, watch television. Roger had hinted recently that it might be a good idea if Hooper was to move in with him until he found a place of his own. Hooper thought he might welcome a firm invitation, even though the Sandringham had become more bearable now he had somewhere to escape to in the week and to take Christopher at weekends. But he didn't want to push Roger. He knew that in some corner of his friend's mind was the hope, though faint and dying, that his wife and son would one day return to him as suddenly as they had gone. To have Hooper move in as a housemate, even only temporarily, would have been to say that hope was dead.

He was in the kitchen preparing the salad. Roger had gone down to the delicatessen on Battersea Rise for ham slices and salami. He heard the front door opening, and then a woman's voice calling 'Ro-ger!' He rested from his work, and stood up, still clutching the Little Devil kitchen knife he had been slicing cucumber with. He heard people moving through the hall. And then Richard appeared in the doorway. He smiled to see Hooper and hurried over.

'Careful with that knife!'

He looked up to see a woman in white denim overalls standing in the doorway. She was frowning in fear at the implement in his hand. He dropped it on the table and put his arm round the little boy.

'I'm perfectly safe,' he said to her distantly.

She smiled then, and looked him over. 'Where's Roger?' she asked.

'Shopping.'

'Ah . . . Look. I have to leave Richard here. I've got a dance class in half an hour.' She frowned as if contemplating the effort she would have to make to get to it. 'My friend was going to look after him but she's had to go to a meeting. So if Roger can take him tonight . . . '

'I'm sure he can,' said Hooper coldly.

The woman nodded, relieved. He supposed that, having got her way, she would be rushing off now to her class. But instead she lingered in the doorway.

'I'm Cheryl,' she said.

'Yes.'

'Are you Bill? I've heard about you.'

'Yes.'

'You're married to that little Emmy Hooper, aren't you?'

'Yes, she is quite small,' he agreed. 'And, yes, she is my wife.'

For the first time he looked at her straight. The photos of her around Roger's house had prepared him for her good looks – the wide, open face, cat-eyes, the mouth broad and humorous, her confident, athletic stance. As she stood there watching him, she rocked gently back and forth, tensing first one leg, then the other. He guessed she didn't know she was doing it. It wasn't as if she was fidgeting, but that she did it for the simple pleasure of feeling her efficient body in motion. Yes, yes – though he thought he loathed everything she stood for – he was not going to deny her attractions. He could scarcely do that – she compelled admiration.

On the other hand . . . looking closer, Hooper saw too, with satisfaction, that there were lines on the face of Cheryl Langford. She was beautiful and proud, but she had lived long enough for there to be these flaws, wrinkles, laughter-lines, blemishes. Underneath her jaunty overalls, he guessed, and in spite of all her dancing and free-expressing, there would be a thickening around the waist, creasing at the hips and buttocks, sag at the breast . . . All was as it should be. Time was grinding down Cheryl Langford too. He felt like rubbing his hands together.

Hooper took a keen and somewhat glutinous interest in the gentle physical decay of his female acquaintances. Sometimes he wondered if it might be a sort of subtle revenge he was enjoying. His own figure was still almost as trim as in his twenties, he had pretty well all his teeth, and hardly any wrinkles except a few attractively, he'd been told, around the mouth. It was true that the other day he had found a grey hair on his head, the first one ever, but –

'Emmy's living with somebody else now, isn't she?' Cheryl enquired.

Hooper opened and closed his mouth.

'Ah well!' She grinned at him matily. 'Life's rich pattern, eh?' She looked him over again approvingly. 'I'm glad Roger's got a friend,' she said. 'I worry about him '

Hooper still had nothing to say.

'Is he all right? He's so quiet, it's hard to know what's going on.'

'He's all right.'

She waited for him to say more. Then, when he didn't, she shrugged. 'Oh well . . . will you ask him to get in touch? I've got something to tell him.'

'Yes.'

She started to go, then looked back at him. 'You're not very forthcoming,' she commented, 'are you?'

'No, I'm not very forthcoming.' How he despised her!

As instructed, he told Roger on his return that his wife wanted to talk to him. Roger was clearly intrigued that the meeting had taken place. He watched Hooper minutely.

'What did you think?' he said at last.

Hooper shrugged.

'She's good-looking, isn't she?' Roger said with wistful pride.

'Yes.' He concentrated on the salad. He was helping Richard grate carrots on to it.

'You can see what a surprise it was . . . when she agreed to live with me.'

Hooper looked up at his friend in irritation and pity. 'I think *she* was bloody lucky,' he said firmly. And he did think this – though in his heart, he realised, he also thought that Roger had indeed done well for himself. And that evening he caught himself more than once speculating on how much better he might have done were it him trying to hang on to Cheryl Langford. It was hard not to think that he might have managed it all much more successfully.

On the way back to Hammersmith he was still thinking about Cheryl. And in bed that night, touching himself, he thought again of her. As she was now, and as she must have been once. For it required no great effort of imagination to see her then, striding forth – brave, free, intelligent, honey-coloured – through some Arcadian 'Sixties summer day. As he stroked himself, he orchestrated a mental sound-track to accompany his visions. Itchycoo Park. Proud Mary. The Devil in Disguise. He was full of the pride he often felt when he thought of the women of his age and how special they had been. Emmy and he used to laugh together about a movie poster they had once seen, long ago. It showed an adulterous older woman in conversation with her much-younger lover, saying of her husband, 'He's got something you'll never have . . . He knew me what I was nineteen!' And it was true: for him, and with all his female friends, he found this knowledge an unbreakable bond.

When he was younger, Hooper had been something of an *aficionado* of the poetry of loss. Parties back in those fabled days had often ended with him lying full-stretch on the carpet, enquiring of captive audiences too drunk, stoned, or weary to protest, the whereabouts of last year's snows. Or tolling forth the noble closing lines of *The Great Gatsby*. Or,

> Time, like an ever-rolling stream
> Bears all its sons away;
> They fly forgotten, as a dream
> Dies at the opening day.

These were all especial favourites of Hooper's, who was not then much aware of the pain concealed in the pretty words. But for all these famous requiems, he thought he had once seen it put just as well by an unknown hand. One summer Emmy and he had lived in a friend's old house in the Catskill Mountains of New York State. Emmy was pregnant with Christopher. It was, he thought suddenly, as he lay in bed, holding himself, their last happy time together. One day, looking along the bookshelves, he had come upon a yearbook from Elmira College, dating from the early 1930s. In it there was an article by what was probably their oldest living alumnus, an old man who had attended the college back in the middle of the previous century when it had been largely a female seminary. At the end of his freshman year, the Civil War had broken out, and he had dropped out of college and gone to enlist in the Union Army. Back in Elmira his classmates, overwhelmingly female as they were, had set to work lovingly and patriotically. So in camp, to the admiration and envy of his comrades, he had been deluged with gifts, tokens, letters, locks of hair, knitted socks, and keepsakes. Now in the 1930s the old soldier looked back over so many years to what must have been the brave, bright peak of his existence. The Elmira girls who had shared it with him were all dead now or scattered, lost forever from his sight at any rate. In the last sentence of his article this old, old man could not contain his feelings of love and loss and pride in his and their memories. 'Oh, where are the darling girls of '64?' he wrote.

Where, oh, where? echoed Hooper in his dingy room in the Sandringham, as the waves of orgasm passed away and sleep drew near and his thoughts turned muzzy and soft. Cheryl Langford . . . He believed he had every reason to scorn and despise the woman. But there was always this bond, this backward tug, always the grail seemed to lie behind him. The present was so little to his liking, and the future held out no hope. No interest. None at all. A year from now, ten years from now – they meant nothing to him. He wouldn't cross the street to see the year 2000. But backwards! – how much sweeter it was to drift on the long receding wave . . .

He had a clear moment of panic then as he realised where his thoughts were taking him. But then his sleepy spirit grumbled resentfully. 'I don't give a shit,' he thought to himself. And then for emphasis muttered it out loud. He would not for one night hold himself back from this enchanted groping and fumbling towards the past. Life was too tough just now, and, for tonight, he didn't give a shit.

9

For many weeks the two men were kind and gentle friends to one another. To Hooper it was clear that the companionship had contributed much to the change that had come over him. It seemed long ago that he had come stumbling bloody-faced and incoherent into the Steins' party, the first time he had seen Roger. He would not do that now. He was ashamed when he looked back on that histrionic performance. And on all the other performances. He felt no urge to repeat them. To outward appearance, he was quite composed and sober now. Within him he was aware vaguely that not much had changed. He still had no communication with Emmy. He had no communication with anyone really, except Roger. He nursed his hurt, and that felt so bad that it stopped him from ever being able to settle down in peace to work out why his life had gone so wrong. So in one sense what he had now was much grimmer, for it seemed to be becoming a settled way of life.

Once in a while, when he felt really bad, he could not help himself breaking into a fresh tirade against the women of his generation. Or against the harmful effects of old movies. Sometimes the two came together.

'Did you ever see *Coming Home*? Jane Fonda, Jon Voight?'

'Yes,' said Roger.

'Wasn't the message of that film that the ideal kind of a man is a loving paraplegic flat on his back?'

'Gosh.' Roger scratched his head. 'I just thought it was about the futility of war.'

Hooper shook his head at his friend's denseness. 'Cannibals,' he muttered, who had once argued for feminism against women. 'The bitches wanted us dead!'

'But remember,' Roger urged. 'You also had films like *Love Story* back then.'

'What's that got to do with it?'

'Well, that was on your side, wasn't it?'

'That's *not* "my side"!' Hooper raged. He glared at Roger suspiciously. He was being incredibly stupid. Sometimes Hooper feared that Roger was poking fun at him subtly. He did not like the thought of that. It seemed very impertinent to him. It also reinforced his belief that there were sides to Roger that he didn't really know about, that Roger took care to keep hidden. In general these incidents had the effect of shutting up Hooper fast.

Anyway such outbreaks were exceptional. Most of the time Hooper's façade was quite convincing, and the sharpest pains were usually held at bay. For this he thanked Roger's friendship. It had brought some order into his life, a point round which he could to some degree collect himself. One Saturday, without feeling that it was a particularly momentous act, he sold his old enemy the

Kawasaki for a quarter of what he paid for it, and bought a second-hand Renault. 'No more spills,' Roger commented, and Hooper hoped it would be so.

The great bond between the two men, of course, was that they shared the terrible experience of threatened fatherhood. This was so, even though they hardly ever spoke directly to each other about the condition. And when they did they used a sort of shorthand, referring to it as 'the disaster' or 'this bloody thing'. Nobody else, Hooper was sure, could understand what it meant to him. Once he went out for a drink with Paul Mosby and at one point, when the conversation had drifted round to his separation from Emmy, he was startled to hear his old friend saying, 'You know, Bill, you've got it made.'

Hooper gaped at the other man. 'I've *what*?'

'I'm talking about the kid,' nodded Paul, who had three of his own. 'I mean, I've got my little sods in my hair morning, noon and night. But there you are – you see your kid exactly when you want to. The rest of the time you're free as a bird.' Paul saluted him with his beer mug. 'Congratulations! . . . Well, come on now,' he added gently, as Hooper continued to stare at him in amazement. 'Didn't you once tell me you were sick and tired of being a bloody child-minder every day of your life?'

'Yes, but – '

'Didn't you say it was like being on a treadmill you couldn't get off?'

'But I didn't mean – '

'Well, now you're off it. So congratulations. Very shrewd of you.'

Hooper was so agitated that he could hardly speak, hardly breathe. 'But you surely don't think – you don't think I *welcome* what's happened?'

Paul watched him, but said nothing.

'You don't think,' Hooper panted, 'I *arranged it*? For God's sake! . . . What do you mean "*shrewd*"?'

'All right. I was kidding – '

'Kidding!'

'All I meant was – it's a rotten situation, but there are some compensations, no?'

'No!'

After a moment Paul sighed and rubbed his eyes. 'OK. Don't get excited.' He looked away then. 'Forget it, Bill.' He rapped on the counter. 'Drink up. I'll buy you another one.'

Hooper was shocked to the core that Paul could make a joke of matters that were so crucial to him. Full of anger, he soon made an excuse to get out of the pub alone. And whenever he looked back on the conversation in the days that followed, it was still always through a screen of anger – which proved a solid defence against any stray anxious thoughts that there might have been an element of sense in Paul's senseless words. In the end, the main lesson he drew from the talk was that he should henceforth confine himself to his friendship with Roger. Roger could be counted on to understand. And to sympathise. And not make silly jokes. Roger was a victim too.

In time perhaps this relationship would have cloyed for him. There was something, he suspected, rather comic and pathetic about the two of them – melancholy bachelors and companions in misfortune, an odd couple with their regrets and reminiscences and the tasty meals they affectionately prepared for each other. It was perhaps a little too bland, this static autumnal mould. He wondered occasionally if in time, a few more months, the friendship would die a gentle, easy, natural death. He was never to know. In the new year, a few weeks after his first encounter with Cheryl Langford, Hooper discovered that the even, restful mood, almost an imitation of serenity, that he and Roger had achieved together was broken for good.

10

It was on a day when he had dropped in at Roger's as usual to prepare the evening meal. He had bought a fresh roasting chicken at the Junction, and was keen to try out a recipe from the new cook book he'd given Roger for Christmas.

Roger was sitting slumped on the sofa in the living-room.

'It'll take a while,' Hooper cried, brandishing the plastic bag that held the chicken. 'But anything extraordinary is worth waiting – '

He stopped. Roger had not moved to welcome him. He was sitting in the middle of a great muddle of empty coffee cups and yesterday's papers. He was wearing jeans and a sweatshirt. His feet were bare and his face unshaved. He looked like he hadn't left the house all day.

'What's up?' Hooper said finally.

Roger looked up. His eyes were bleared with misery. 'I talked to Cheryl last night.'

'And?'

'She's going away. She's taking Richard.'

He came and sat beside his friend on the cluttered sofa.

'Where's she going?'

'Australia.'

While Hooper stared at him, Roger rubbed his tired eyes. 'That's where her friend comes from. Jeannie . . . They're going . . . Sydney. Perth . . . I don't know. Somewhere.' He shrugged his shoulders helplessly at the enormity of the Australian continent, the vastness of his misery.

'When is she going?'

'I don't know . . . Soon. She needs a visa . . . It should be easy. Jeannie's family'll help her . . . Oh Christ,' Roger fretted vaguely. 'I should have gone into school today. There's a meeting. But I just felt I . . . She's going to let me have Richard for a whole week before they go. And we talked about me maybe flying out there to visit at

Easter . . . ' He rocked to and fro in his distress.

'Bitch!' Hooper exploded. 'Dirty, twisting bitch!'

Roger looked up, feebly angry. 'I warned you, Bill – '

'Oh, stuff it! She walks in here, out of the blue, and calmly tells you – '

'She wasn't calm. She was quite upset for me. She almost cried . . . and Cheryl never cries,' said Roger, sad and wondering. 'And it wasn't out of the blue. I've known she was thinking about it since October.'

'Since *October*!' Hooper was amazed, wounded. 'Why didn't you tell me?'

'I don't know . . . I thought it would go away. But it hasn't . . . Oh God.' He put his arms over his head in his sorrow.

It required no thought for Hooper to know what to do. As if it was a role he had long been preparing for and knew by heart. 'Get him,' he said. Still without thinking he sank to his knees before his friend's huddled body. Roger looked up in surprise. 'Get him away from her,' Hooper insisted. 'Christ's sake, you have to.'

'Get him away?' Roger's expression was shocked, absolutely. 'Take him away from her?'

'Yes.'

'How can I? She's his *mother*.'

'And you're his *father* . . . There's no alternative,' Hooper cried, grabbing at the material that covered the sofa in his insistence. 'What else can you do? Are you just going to give him up? Without a fight? Do you think you can *replace* him?'

Roger winced at the thought. Hooper kept on at him. 'She's torn it down. Whatever arrangement you thought you had, she's destroyed it. It's just you and her now, and one of you's got to win. Why should it be her? *Why*?'

After a moment Roger said, 'What can I do? How can I get him? What – steal him? Run away to the Continent?'

'Of course not,' said Hooper impatiently. 'Do it legally.'

'What?'

'Legally. Get custody of him.'

'But we're not divorced yet.'

'You don't have to be. I'm sure you don't . . . Get custody,' he urged. 'Get the bloody law on your side. That'd make her think a bit, wouldn't it?' he glowed. 'Eh?'

But Roger was shaking his head. 'I couldn't take Cheryl to court.'

'You probably wouldn't have to,' said Hooper excitedly. 'All you need is a solicitor's letter saying you're applying for custody. She'd crumple up straight away . . . Yes!' he cried, for Roger was still shaking his head. 'That's how people do it . . . Look. When Creighton – Creighton Phillips – I told you about him – at work – when he was fooling around more than usual, his wife – his second wife . . . ' Hooper stopped. He was getting tangled up and he had to get this right. He started again, carefully. 'She took the kids off to her mother's one weekend. Next thing that happened was that Creighton got a letter from a solicitor. Very formal. Very hard-nose. Details of separation arrangements. She to get custody of the children. Him to pay so much a week for support. Creighton told me it was the shock of his life when he read that letter. Sobered him up completely. He went crawling to her . . . And I talked to her later. She said she'd only done it to jerk his lead a bit. And it worked. That's how people *do it*, Roger. That's what you've got to do. Jerk her lead a bit,' he repeated, relishing the phrase.

But for a long time Roger wouldn't even consider it. Long into the evening Hooper wrestled the question with his friend. He painted the likely loneliness of Roger's childless future. He forced on him the idea that it would be no different than if Richard had died. And that by his acquiescence, so supine, Roger in a manner was contributing to that death. 'Stop this suffering Jesus act, will you?' he bawled at one point. 'Wake up!' Did Roger not want Richard? Was that it? Was he secretly relieved to be letting go of the burden of his son?

'You know I'm not!' Roger cried out in fury.

'Then fucking fight for him!' Hooper roared, inwardly pleased to see his friend's anger rising up at last. 'Otherwise who's going to fucking believe it?'

Around nine o'clock, Roger said at last, 'All right. All right. I'd do it . . . But don't you see? You need grounds for custody – '

'For a solicitor's letter. That's all. A tough bloody letter.'

'Even for that. You need grounds. Or else it's just empty threats . . . and I haven't got any grounds.'

After that Hooper was silent. He sat and stared at the carpet. Roger got up from the sofa. He picked up the chicken in its bag. 'It's too late to cook this,' he said dully. 'I'm going to scramble some eggs. Want some?'

Hooper looked up. 'I'll tell you what . . . ' An idea was forming in his mind, opening up perfectly like a rose. 'I heard Sam Stein talking about a case one day,' he said slowly. An excellent idea! 'You know, I'm not sure, but I think you might have grounds . . . I think it's worth a try anyway.'

11

The choice of solicitor proved difficult. It struck Hooper as strange, or rather as a mark of culpable innocence, that in their thirties, having lived so long, neither of them had the name of a smart, aggressive lawyer ready to hand. Of course, they both had friends who were lawyers, and Hooper was on good terms with Joe Sanderson who ran the legal department at Overton's but, hardly discussing it, they agreed not to bring any of them in on this. It was something to be done with strangers. In the end, Roger suggested going to the firm on Lavender

Hill that had handled the conveyancing on his house, and Hooper could think of no better alternative.

'I suppose it doesn't matter really,' he said uncertainly. 'I mean, it's all the same law.'

At one point Roger asked him to come along to the interview to give him support. It had not occurred to Hooper that he wouldn't be involved all the way in the proceedings, so he was happy to agree. Things were quiet at the office, and he was well able to take time off to pursue this righteous venture. And Roger's school fortunately was still on holiday.

'So we've got nothing else to think about,' said Hooper, in the tones of a soccer-club manager at half-time. 'Just this.'

'Right', agreed Roger, a little nervously. 'God', he sighed. 'She's going to be so *angry*.'

Hooper looked at his friend doubtfully. The thought that Roger might back down on this was a constant fear. 'Australia,' he reminded him tersely.

'Yes.' Roger nodded and tried to look determined. 'Yes, I know.'

Their appointment with the solicitor was at four o'clock, a Friday afternoon. After a short wait in a bare outer room, they were ushered into the presence of a woman, younger than themselves, dressed in a trim, dark business-outfit. She looked cool and competent. Roger explained that he would like to have his friend sit in on the interview, and she nodded as if this was nothing unusual.

She took down a few details. Roger and Cheryl's marriage. The birth of their child. The wife's exit from the family home, taking the little boy with her.

'And now you wish to apply for custody?'

'Uh – yes. Sort of.' Roger glanced back to where Hooper had taken a seat a little way behind him. Hooper nodded encouragingly.

'On what grounds?'

'Er . . . she's a lesbian.'

The solicitor looked at Roger for a moment, and then made a note on her pad. 'Practising?'

'What? . . . Oh. Yes. She is.'

'How long have you known this?'

'Oh, for ages.'

'Before you were married?'

'Yes.'

'While you were married?'

'Right.'

The solicitor laid down her pen. 'So you might be said, Mr Miles, to have condoned her behaviour throughout.'

Roger stared at the woman. Who then asked, 'Did you condone it?'

Roger wriggled wretchedly in his seat. He looked back again at Hooper – but Hooper couldn't help him. 'I suppose so,' he said at last.

'Yes,' said the woman gravely. 'I'm thinking, you see, that in the face of what you've just told me, if this ever came to court a judge might have great difficulty distinguishing between yourself and your wife on moral grounds. The danger being, of course, that he might conclude that the best course of action with regard to the child – whose interests will come first with him – would be to place him in the care of the local authority.'

'Christ!' They both gazed at her in horror.

She looked thoughtfully back at them. And then, in tones that were both practical and kind, she said, 'In these cases I almost always urge my clients to exhaust every avenue of compromise before they go to law . . . And in your case, Mr Miles,' she concluded, 'I think you'd be mad not to.'

They walked back in silence across the Common which was covered now in a rare heavy fall of snow. Hooper felt utterly defeated. The world, he saw again in all clarity, was a cold, remorseless place. Injustice ruled and the weak submitted. They passed near where an asphalt hill, long and low like a burial mound, protruded out of the soil of the Common. Hooper had once told Roger fancifully that this was the dome of a bomb-shelter cannily prepared far beneath the earth by the governing élite of South London against the outbreak of the Third World War. The little boys had often mountaineered on this hill and raced their tricycles on it. He felt a stab of pain to see it now, a lump under the snow. Christopher's playmate would soon be gone, far away, and no hand could stay the miserable process.

12

In the living-room of Roger's house, he tried to rouse himself to play the comforter. 'I'm sorry,' he began wearily. 'I really am so sorry . . . ' He talked at his friend like this for at least a minute before he realised that Roger wasn't listening. He also saw that he had no idea at all what was going on inside his friend's head. Once in Mexico City, when Emmy and he were travelling, an earth tremor had shook the city. It took time for the English couple, who knew of these things only by legend, to pin-point exactly what was happening. They were walking in a park in the centre of town, when they saw people around them pointing agitatedly. Some of them sank to their knees and began praying. Then they saw that the water in a small pond nearby was sliding back and forth and lapping over the edge. Then the high buildings around the park, they saw, were swaying like flowers in a breeze, and chunks of tile and glass were falling off. And still it took seconds more before they could understand what all these signs added up to. Ah! Yes! This is an *earthquake*. Of course . . .

So now with Roger. The slow burning of his anger. The pacing up and down. Even to the moment when he grabbed a vase from the little table by the door and hurled it at the mirror over the mantelpiece. Roger at last was showing all that was buried within him – but Hooper could not grasp what these portents indicated. He stared at the glass that lay shattered in a broad spray on the carpet. His mind was groping forward . . .

'Fuck it!' cried Roger, who hardly ever swore. 'I'm not finished!'

Hooper watched astounded as his friend prowled fiercely round the room.

'Honestly,' Hooper started nervously. 'I think she was giving you good advice. Compromise – '

'How can I compromise? She's taking him to *Australia*.'

'But you've told her now,' Hooper explained. 'You said you knew Cheryl was gay all along – '

'All right!' Roger roared. 'And now I'll find another bloody lawyer and I'll say something different.'

Hooper was shocked to hear that – and it was a long time before he understood exactly why he reacted this way. Now he only blurted out naîvely, 'But that's dishonest!'

'Oh dear!' his friend sneered. 'Is it?' He jutted out his powerful jaw. 'I'm going through with this. To the bloody end. Jesus!' He started to stride once again up and down the room. 'I sat there in front of that damn woman, making a fool of myself, and I suddenly thought – you creep! Your kid's slipping away from you and you're doing nothing to stop it. Nothing! . . . You're right, Bill. You're so right . . . These *women*. They want us dead. I *am* dead, and I never even knew it . . . He's mine!' he shouted. 'He's my *son* . . . *Cheryl* . . . Australia!' He brought one great fist smashing down on the table where the vase had once rested. It crumpled beneath the blow. He stared lividly at Hooper, who took a frightened step backward. 'What's Sam Stein's number?' he demanded. 'I'm going to get the best fucking lawyer there is.' He walked over to the phone. He glared back at Hooper. 'Fuck it, Bill! What's his number?'

All at once Hooper felt himself swept up into the

orther's rage. It was tremendous, irresistible, like a scorching gale, sweeping away all the little issues of propriety and fair play.

'You're right!' he cried. 'We'll get that letter written.'

'Sod letters,' said Roger grimly. 'I'm going all the way. I'm getting custody.'

They stared at each other across the room. Hooper swallowed . . . and then he thought: Yes. Yes! Roger was right. Why tiptoe around any more? All the way. The killer thrust.

He felt great. He felt like a pirate. He crossed the room and took the phone from his friend's hand.

'I'll ring him. You stay out of it for a bit.'

After a moment Roger nodded, and Hooper dialled Sam Stein's home. 'He may be working,' he muttered to Roger. 'But Sally'll give us his office number.'

But he was at home. 'Hi, Bill.'

'Sam,' Hooper said earnestly. 'Who's the best solicitor there is? For getting custody?'

There was a pause at the other end. Then Sam sighed. 'Bill,' he started patiently, 'honestly, you haven't got much of a chance – '

'It's not for me,' Hooper snapped. 'It's for a friend.'

There was nothing from the other end. Hooper gripped the phone tightly. 'I swear it, Sam. It's for a friend.'

'Well, all right,' said Sam Stein reluctantly at last. Then, 'Jane Powell's the best. No question.'

'Great.' Hooper looked around for a pencil. 'Have you got her office number?'

'Yeah. Somewhere.' There was silence at the other end. Hooper took a pencil from Roger and waited. Sam's voice came back, a little hesitant. 'Er . . . Bill – could I ask? Is this friend of yours a man or a woman?'

'He's a man.'

'Ah . . . no luck then. Janey won't act for a man in a custody case. Anything else, but she draws the line at that.'

'It's a conspiracy!' Hooper raged when he had got over the shock. 'It's a stinking fix!'

He felt then the pained silence from the other end. Also Roger was watching him, irritated and puzzled. He mastered himself. 'All right,' he said into the receiver. 'Who else is there? There must be somebody good.'

'There's lots,' said Sam Stein. A pause. Then, 'Are you looking for somebody with – you know – the right attitude? Somebody who thinks like us?'

'Sam . . . ' Hooper held his forehead. 'Sam, all I want is somebody who wins a lot of custody cases. I don't care about anything else.'

'Oh. I see,' said Sam Stein in a disappointed tone. He seemd to ponder a little more. Then, 'There's a firm called Manners, Scruby – somewhere near Bond Street. Get hold of Leonard Scruby.'

'Scruby.' Hooper wrote it down. 'Have you got the number?'

'Be in the book. Manners, Scruby, W1 . . . But you know, Bill, I'm not sure you're going to like him.'

'That'll be my misfortune,' Hooper said, anxious now to hang up.

'Yes . . . And if I could pass on a word of advice to your *friend*. Before he goes to law, he really should explore every avenue of – '

'Thanks, Sam. We know all about that.'

13

'And you had no idea that your wife was subject to these tendencies?'

'None whatsoever,' said Roger firmly.

Seated in a comfortable swivel armchair behind his friend, Hooper nodded approvingly. There had been plenty of time over the weekend for Roger to rehearse for this interview, and it was going extremely well. Hooper felt he could afford to relax and let himself take in his surroundings. Except for the disaster on Lavender Hill, the only other lawyers' offices that he had been in belonged to his friends, and they were always dusty, cramped, ill-lit environments, whose walls were drably decorated with legal-aid posters, anti-police brutality petitions, advertisements for group holidays in the socialist democracies. Leonard Scruby's office was quite different from these. It was sleek and spacious. There was a wealth of potted palms, light furniture, thick-pile carpet. Venetian blinds controlled the influx of sunlight. Double-glazed windows blotted out the snarl of traffic from Bond Street below. When neither lawyer nor client was speaking, there was no sound in the room, except for an occasional faint rustle as Scruby turned a page of his notebook and, distantly, the insistent melodies of Andrew Lloyd Webber, drifting in from loudspeakers hidden in the luxurious waiting-room outside.

'And how did you discover your wife's proclivities?'

'My son told me.'

'Richard? Aged four?'

'Yes.'

'Excellent,' murmured Leonard Scruby. 'What did he tell you?'

'That she's sharing a bed with this woman.'

'Who is a lesbian?'

'Oh, yes.' Roger thought for a moment. 'Jeannie got married once. To another woman.'

Scruby looked up. 'Married?'

'They went through a ceremony. There's a cutting about it from *Gay News* at home somewhere . . . I don't know if she ever got divorced.'

'This is all extremely promising,' Leonard Scruby commented, apparently to himself, writing steadily away.

Roger looked back to Hooper and smiled. Hooper returned the smile, and then looked past his friend to study the lawyer. On this, his first descent into the world of slick, unscrupulous legal sharks, he had been a little disappointed when he first met Leonard Scruby. 'Family-man' was the tag he immediately put on him. Scruby looked to be in his late forties, a small, burly man, with a large head. He was bald except for a fringe of curly black hair around his ears and the back of his skull. He had greeted Roger and Hooper with diffident friendliness. His smile was warm, but anxious too, as if seeking their approval. And Scruby's accent . . . though Hooper would never use the word, his mother, he knew, would have had to call it 'common'. Just slightly. But noticeably.

Hooper looked again around the room, trying to connect its black aura with its homely occupant. On a low table beneath the window was a row of signed photographs. They were too far away for him to be able to read the signatures. They were not exactly famous faces, but they seemed familiar all the same. One, he thought, might be a politician. Another, he was almost certain, hosted a late-night TV show, a medical programme, or religious, something like that.

From outside came the strains of 'Take That Look Off Your Face'. On another table, beneath another window, as if sternly separated from the celebrities, were what he took to be the family portraits: a photo of a stout, attractive, smiling woman with streaked dark hair; another of a miniature poodle sitting up and begging; another of a young boy, wearing a school cap and blazer and a very sweet smile.

'Where has your wife taken the boy?' Scruby asked Roger.

'She's living in Brixton now.'

'Excellent', murmured the solicitor yet again, and bent over his notes. Roger winked at Hooper. Cheryl and Richard were presently living in a salubrious quarter known as Poets Corner from the names of the surrounding roads: Chaucer, Spenser, Shakespeare, Milton. For neighbours they had on one side two doctors, husband

and wife, and on the other a man who worked for Current Affairs at London Weekend Television.

Scruby laid down his golden ball-point. He gave Roger one of his quick, nervous smiles, and then his features settled into an expression of great gravity. He cleared his throat. 'Well, obviously this is an exceedingly serious situation.' Roger nodded. 'And I think,' the lawyer added, 'that action should be taken without delay.'

'Well . . . I agree,' Roger breathed.

'Now you appreciate that it is the *child's* welfare that will be the court's first consideration? In these matters we are governed by the Guardianship of Minors Act of 1971. In the old days,' Scruby reminisced, 'we were much more concerned with the concept of the guilty party. No longer. The fact that it was your wife who chose to leave the matrimonial home, the fact that she has now embarked on a sexual liaison outside the marriage – these are by themselves of no consequence beside the paramount importance placed on the interests of the child.'

There was silence in the room. Scruby seemed to be collecting his thoughts. Hooper was none too sure where these comments had left them. The lawyer's next statement deepened his fears.

'Now ordinarily a judge would probably consider the enforced removal of the child from the care of one parent to that of the other an act which, for the child's sake, could only be justified in the most extreme circumstances.'

'I see,' sighed Roger dolefully.

But then the lawyer brightened magically. 'Fortunately, these *are* extreme circumstances. In view of the grave moral danger in which your son is placed. Even though,' he added, 'lesbianism is not and never has been considered a criminal activity.' He smiled benignly then at the whimsicality of the law.

After a moment, Roger nodded. 'Yes?'

'Yes. Now what I propose,' Scruby continued, 'is that we avail ourselves immediately of expert opinion.'

There was some confusion among his hearers. Roger

stared back at Hooper, who shrugged helplessly. 'I thought,' Roger said hesitantly, 'that that was what we were doing.'

Leonard Scruby shook his large head and smiled. 'You need an advocate, Mr Miles. You need a barrister – a good one.'

'I see,' said Roger at length. 'Right,' he nodded.

Scruby thought for a moment. 'At this point,' he resumed, 'I think I should bring up the matter of costs.'

'Costs?'

The lawyer smiled. 'In law as in most things we get what we pay for. Now I should like you, Mr Miles, to get the very best. And barristers who specialise in this particular area . . . ' Scruby paused, then chuckled. 'Well, there's a pecking order in these matters, of course, and the sort of chap we're looking for considers himself pretty high up the ladder. Most of them spend much of their time adjusting details of very large property settlements where there has been a breakdown in a marriage. Now at the present time we aren't concerned with a settlement of property . . . ' He looked down and scanned the notes where at the beginning of the interview, Hooper remembered suddenly, he had carefully listed all Roger's possessions. 'And in any case,' Scruby noted, 'we are not dealing here with very large assets, are we? Nevertheless, if we want a chap of high calibre, we can't expect him to accept less than the usual fee he would charge for his services.'

'I see,' nodded Roger. 'And – er . . . what would that be?'

Leonard Scruby thought for a moment. 'With a bit of luck we might get away with six hundred pounds.'

'Six hun- !'

'Per diem.'

For several moments there was a hushed silence in the room. Then Roger, with effort, collected himself. 'And how many days . . . ?'

'I couldn't say,' the lawyer signed. Then, as if taking

pity, 'I should count on a minimum of three, perhaps four.'

Silence again. Scruby rubbed his eyes and smiled considerately. 'Then there are the other fees . . . My fees.'

'It's just,' Roger faltered after a time. 'I'm a bit broke at the moment . . . We upped the mortgage last year and – '

'Of course,' the lawyer nodded sympathetically. He glanced at his watch. 'It's best for you to be very clear on all this before you get too deeply into it.' He closed his notebook. The interview was clearly moving speedily towards a close. 'The law can be an expensive business,' he nodded. 'I always advise my clients to explore every possible – '

Hooper leaned forward in his seat. 'It's all right.' He exchanged a glance with Roger. 'It's OK,' he said. He looked at the lawyer then. 'We can afford it.'

Leonard Scruby studied Hooper for a moment. Then he nodded cheerfully. 'Very well.' He opened his notebook once again, found his place, picked up his pen. 'I should like to see if we can persuade Mr Varda to appear for us – '

'*Mark* Varda?'

He looked at Hooper again. 'Yes?'

'We know him. At least, we've met him.' He glanced at Roger. 'Sam Stein's. That lunch.'

Roger nodded. The lawyer looked from one friend to the other. 'Well – that won't prove an obstacle, will it? I mean . . . ' He chuckled richly. 'You're not at daggers drawn, I hope?'

Roger shook his head. 'It'll be all right.'

'Good.' The lawyer looked at them earnestly. 'He really is very able. One of the best of the younger men. In fact, I think we're lucky to catch him just in time. He'll be taking silk within a year or two, I'm sure of it.'

Through his secretary Leonard Scruby made the appointment. Mr Varda was presently in court, but would be available to meet for a conference at 2.15, a couple of hours away.

14

To fill the time, the two friends went and had lunch at a sandwich bar in South Molton Street. They both felt excited and hopeful after the interview. Roger was concerned though about the lawyers' fees.

'I can't let you pay for them,' he protested.

'I wasn't planning to. Not all of them. How much can you raise?'

'About five hundred . . . Maybe a thousand.'

'All right. I'll pay anything above that.'

Roger bit into his corned beef sandwich. Then, 'It's ridiculous!' He swallowed, drank coffee. 'I'd pay anything for Richard. Anything at all. I'd sell the house.'

'Don't sell the house,' Hooper advised. 'I've got money sitting around. I'll pay. And you can pay me back.'

'With interest?' Roger gleamed.

'You bet!'

They cackled merrily together. Hooper was in grand spirits, had been feeling very cheerful since he'd got up in the morning with the prospect of the interview with Leonard Scruby before him. It was the promise, now confirmed, that things were moving at last. A bit of power, a whisper of hope coming back into his life after so many defeats. He had to stop himself at moments to remember that this was about Roger's child, and not his own. But it didn't matter. He felt good all the same. It had even allowed him to have a quite pleasant moment with Emmy on the pay phone at the Sandringham before he left for the lawyer's office. She had rung up to ask him if he could pick up Christopher from school tomorrow. She had to go somewhere, nobody else was free. He'd said of course, it was no problem. There had been a flicker of affection between them before she'd rung off. 'You're a good father,' she had told him.

'What about Varda though?' said Roger anxiously, as they looked for a taxi to take them to the Temple. 'He seemed a bit of a prick at that lunch, didn't he?'

'I think,' said Hooper seriously, 'a prick is just what we need at this moment.'

Before they'd left his office, Leonard Scruby had raised the matter of Hooper's attendance at the forthcoming conference. 'I'm perfectly happy for you to be there, Mr . . . '

'Hooper,' Hooper reminded him.

'Hooper . . . ' He glanced at Roger. 'If my client so wishes. But I can't, you understand, speak for Mr Varda.'

Mark Varda, though, accepted Hooper's presence in his chambers with no more than a shrug. However, he ignored him completely thereafter, while greeting Roger and shaking hands with him with great ease and friendliness.

'We met at the Steins', didn't we?'

They chatted for a little while about Sam and Sally while Hooper found his usual place in the background. Leonard Scruby settled into one of two chairs placed in front of the desk. Eventually, Mark Varda went and sat behind the desk and indicated that Roger should sit in the other chair. In the interval since the interview with Scruby, the solicitor's notes on the case had been typed up and sent over to Varda's chambers by messenger. The barrister now took a moment to read them through again.

Hooper was glad for the opportunity to study him – and very impressed by what he saw. At the Stein's he had been so busy watching Roger that he had hardly done more than register Mark Varda's presence. 'Swarthy' would have been as much as he could have said if asked to give a description. Perhaps 'tall' he might have been able to add after thought. And then at lunch Varda had been wearing just jeans and sweater, and had clearly not shaved for Sunday. But to look at him now! In his elegant black jacket and high starched white collar with the barrister's necktie resting on a soft, grey-striped shirt. And the face – not swarthy at all. It glowed, darkly pink with good health. His cheeks were impeccably smooth, probably, Hooper guessed, after the day's second shave. No, not swarthy – *saturnine*, perhaps. The black, glossy hair and the hard, bright, dark eyes. There was an air about him, a crisp outline of superiority, a flavour, faintly erotic, somewhere between the perfect school captain and a *Wehrmacht* intelligence officer of the highest calibre. Hooper felt his hopes rise higher with every moment he looked at him.

Varda looked up at the solicitor. 'Quick smash-and-grab in the county court would get my vote, Leonard.'

Leonard Scruby nodded as if he'd been expecting the judgment. 'You wouldn't consider the magistrates?'

The barrister frowned and shook his head. 'I really find them so unreliable. No . . . ' He nodded firmly. 'I'd much rather take my chances before a judge.' He thought for a moment. 'Before the *right* judge.' He flicked a switch on the little communication box on his desk.

'Mr Varda?' came a man's voice, Cockney accent.

'Harry,' said Mark Varda pleasantly, 'will you find out who's sitting at Battersea this afternoon.'

They waited for a while in silence. Hooper noticed that Varda's dark eyes seemed brilliant with suppressed excitement, as if he was concealing a delicious secret. Finally, he confessed. 'Leonard,' he said. 'I've bought a new boat. Sixty foot.'

Scruby smiled in admiration. 'Picked it up cheap,' the barrister exulted. 'Firm was going bust.'

'Where is she?' Scruby asked.

'On the Hamble . . . I'm going to take her out to Barbados in July. If I can get away.'

'Do you need any crew?'

'Want to come along?'

'I'm thinking of my son. I'm sure an ocean trip would be so good for Neville . . . ' The solicitor stopped, seemed to ponder his words. 'The physical challenge,' he suggested in doubtful tones.

'Sure.' Mark Varda made a note on top of the type-written pages that concerned the case of Roger Miles. 'Will you give me a ring after Easter?'

The communication box buzzed. Varda flipped the switch. 'Yes, Harry?'

'Judge Kirby-Smith is sitting this afternoon, Mr Varda.'

'Terrific!' The barrister beamed across the desk. Scruby looked up at the low ceiling of Varda's burrow-like room and chuckled. 'Well, that *is* convenient,' the barrister grinned. 'Kirby-Smith! What is he, Leonard? Roman?'

'*Anglo*-Catholic, I thought.'

'Something handy anyway . . . Though actually you wouldn't have known it when he was at the bar. He seemed a perfectly normal, reasonable sort of fellow.'

'Well, one's seen that happen often enough,' Scruby commented.

The two lawyers nodded together. Then they seemed to recall the presence of the laymen. Mark Varda stood up. 'I'll go and feed Harry the details, see if we can get in to see him this afternoon.' He crossed the room swiftly and exited. Leonard Scruby turned to Roger beside him – with a sideways flick of his eyes he barely included Hooper – and began to translate for them.

'What Mr Varda has in mind – and I quite agree with him – is an *ex parte* application before a county court judge. What that means is that we will appear before the judge in chambers and apply to him to make an order directing your wife to surrender care and control of your child. We'll be going to Battersea as that is the court that has jurisdiction in the area where you live. We'll explain to the judge the reasons why we think it absolutely vital for the child to be removed from the mother's care – her lesbianism, in fact . . . Now we have good reason to hope that the particular judge who is sitting there this afternoon

– if we can get in to see him – may take a serious view of your wife's behaviour. So if we're reasonably fortunate we should be able to serve an order on her and get possession of the child by the end of the afternoon.'

There was a moment's tense silence, and then Roger said, in faintly shocked tones, 'But doesn't Cheryl have to be there too?'

'Your wife?' The solicitor shook his head. 'It's an *ex parte* application,' he explained. 'Only the applicants need be present.'

'But can you do that?' Hooper cried out involuntarily. 'Sorry,' he said awkwardly, as the solicitor frowned impatiently at him.

Scruby turned back to his client. 'Now you understand that should we get it, it will only be a temporary order. Within a period – probably seven days – we'll have to go back before the judge to substantiate our claims. And your wife will then be able to make an appearance and produce whatever counter-claims and arguments she wants. It won't be over today by a long chalk,' he warned.

'But I could have Richard living with me by this evening?' said Roger, wondering.

'Perhaps,' smiled the solicitor. 'But it's not certain, by any means.'

'It all seems very easy.'

'Pardon?'

'It's just . . . ' Roger hestiated. 'I thought the law was so slow.'

'Oh, it can be,' nodded Scruby. 'It certainly can be . . . But where there's a fire, one mustn't delay the fire brigade. *We* are the fire brigade,' he explained.

The door swung open. Mark Varda appeared, smiling triumphantly. 'We're on!' he crowed. 'Quarter past three.' He glanced at his watch. 'Should make it. If the traffic's kind.'

15

It was. There was a jam on the turn-off on to Waterloo Bridge, but after that their taxi had a clear run along Albert Embankment and then all the long way up Wandsworth Road. Leonard Scruby spent part of the journey scribbling on a sheet of paper that rested on the side of his rigid attaché case. When he'd finished, he passed it to the barrister who read it quickly and nodded and gave it to Roger.

'It's your affidavit,' Scruby explained. 'It sets out your reasons for applying for care and control. The judge will probably want Mr Varda to go through them orally, but he'll want a bit of paper in front of him too. I think we've got everything in there, haven't we?' Roger nodded.

Mark Varda seemed to want to talk quite a lot as they sped along. It didn't appear exactly that he was apprehensive – more that he was encouraging himself, stirring up his adrenalin, rehearsing all the reasons why he could not possibly fail. 'I think Kirby-Smith'll be all right,' he said to Scruby at one point.

'Oh, I think so.'

'Though five years from now it might be a different story,' the barrister sighed. 'The courts are changing their views about lesbian mothers,' he explained to his client. 'Outside London they still take a pretty dim view, but these city judges – well, it's getting a bit dicey . . . ' He glanced again at Leonard Scruby. 'I know Jane Powell has won a couple of custody cases for lesbians lately.'

'So I believe.'

'But I'm sure we'll be OK,' Varda nodded to himself. 'Kirby-Smith's such an old bugger . . . *Young* bugger,' he amended himself. 'How old would you say he was?' he asked his colleague.

'Forty-five?' hazarded Scruby.

'So, we're safe with him for twenty years. Maybe . . . Oh, he'll be all right,' repeated Mark Varda confidently.

The taxi seemed to Hooper to be humming along like a

racing-car. He felt dazed by the speed at which everything was happening today. Beside him, Scruby was checking through the affidavit again. Hooper glanced at the scribbled page. It seemed a frail support on which to rest such great hopes. He feared suddenly that they were only hurrying towards some awful disappointment.

For relief from these thoughts, he turned from Scruby to look out of the window. The familiar sights of his own old neighbourhood were appearing around him. They were at North Street, then the Queenstown Road, Lavender Hill . . . It was strange seeing it from this vantage point, in this company. It was, in fact, a strange-seeming neighbourhood, he saw. On one side of the street there were Pakistani groceries, tumbledown garages, Kentucky Fried, Space Invaders. On the other: chic little wine bars, antique shops, La Crêperie restaurant, a health food store. There were stringy old men out there and huge fat women clutching bulging plastic shopping-bags, and angry young mothers dragging chains of squalling children. And moving among these squat, grey people there were other taller figures, male and female, often agreeably sun-tanned though it was deep winter, clad in furs and down-jackets and long leather coats, stepping smartly out of late-registration Volvos and BMWs, nipping in and out of the speciality stores.

But the scene was dominated by young people, scores of them, black and white, who roamed the narrow pavements in raucous gangs, often forcing everybody else off into the road to make way for them. Hooper looked out at these young folk without affection. He knew he rather detested the generation they belonged to. It was bad. He was ashamed of it. He had many advantages, made money, had grown up in an easier time. They were poor and powerless and, by their own account, were not having much fun out of their youth. Perhaps it was a pose of theirs. Perhaps not. Anyway, he should be more generous. But there it was. Basically he did not trust anybody under thirty. Depressing, they seemed to him. Unappealing. Aggressive. Unnecessary.

It was not much different with the middle-class youngsters at work. He tried to be friendly with the young people of Editorial in their brief passage through Overton's. He didn't find it easy. They seemed strange to him. Old-fashioned in a way, as if they somehow pre-dated him and his friends. Full of conventional anxieties – though it was true that life in Overton's editorial department was a perfect breeder of anxiety. But he could not get a fix on them, could not work out what they stood for. Probably for nothing, collectively. Perhaps, he thought, they were smart not to operate as his own generation had done, thundering around all together, like an animal herd. Only they didn't seem particularly individualistic to him, just isolated.

But at least they didn't fill him with fears for his physical safety as did those kids now out on the street. It was odd. When he had been young it had been an article of faith that violence was the detestable legacy of the older generation. It was strange to have to switch in mid-life and see it as the property of youth, of all the armies of Terry T and Danny T . . .

Once, round at Kenny and Anthea's, when he had been running on like this, Anthea had stopped him by saying, 'Tell me something, Bill – have any of these kids ever actually attacked you?'

'Me? Personally? No.'

'Have they ever even *threatened* you?'

'Er – not really.'

'Well, what on earth are you moaning about, then?'

But the menace in the air could not be denied. Passing between the rows of little shops, he remembered suddenly how they had looked a few months back all boarded-up against the threat of riot. A roadside poster loomed up, demanding, white letters on black, 'How would you like to get your face smashed in?' They were past it before Hooper realised it was only recommending the wearing of car safety-belts.

He looked across at his friend, who smiled in response. 'How do you feel?' he murmured. Roger considered for a moment, then smiled again. 'I feel excited!' he said in slightly surprised tones. Hooper nodded and grinned. He wanted Roger to know that he was with him, every step of the way. But in truth he wasn't sure he could so precisely define what he himself was feeling. Except confused.

The taxi whipped on through the light traffic. They passed the Arts Centre and then the police station. Hooper had thought their destination would be the court-house on Lavender Hill that shared the same square modern building with the police. But Scruby explained, as the taxi went by it, that that was the magistrates court. The county court, to which they were headed, was in an older building beyond the Junction. Once inside, Mark Varda hurried off to speak to the listings officer. The other three stood around in a lobby crowded with uniformed police and uniformed barristers and many people like themselves in ordinary dress. There was a great deal of apprehensive cigarette smoking going on, though Hooper supposed that not everyone there was up for trial. Some of them must be detectives or witnesses or simply members of the public. He looked around surreptitiously trying to work out what was what, and saw that those he spied on were watching his own group with the same shifty interest.

Leonard Scruby was smiling comfortingly up at his client. 'We can leave it all to Mr Varda now,' he promised.

'I intend to!' Roger laughed. Hooper watched his friend with interest and admiration. He had not seen Roger like this before. He seemed nervous, of course, but beautifully alive. Shining. Looking at him, Hooper felt his own spirits rising too. The confusion he had experienced in the taxi melted away. He was supremely glad to be here. What had Scruby called them? – the fire brigade? It was not enough, not for such a romatic adventure as this. They were the 7th Cavalry at least, rising on the crest above the shattered town, and storming down, pennants flying, on their errand of justice and mercy and –

'We're on,' Mark Varda announced, hurrying up. He led the others down a dim corridor to an unmarked door. There he paused and gave his client a quick inspection. 'Tie's loose,' he murmured.

Roger straightened it.

'Right,' nodded Mark Varda. He opened the door. Roger went in, followed by Scruby. Hooper was following after them, when Varda placed a hand on his chest.

'It's in camera,' he stated.

'What?'

'No spectators.'

Varda went into the room and closed the door. Hooper stood there for a few moments gazing at the shut door. Then he walked slowly back down the corridor. In the lobby he looked at his watch. It was seventeen minutes past three.

16

At twenty-six minutes past three, the others reappeared in the lobby. Mark Varda was the first to reach Hooper. He was smiling broadly. 'Very smooth,' he announced.

Hooper turned to Roger who came up next. 'Is it all right?'

Roger nodded without speaking.

'How did it go?'

'Very smooth.' Roger seemed abstracted.

'I must dash,' Varda told Leonard Scruby. 'I've got a conference at four.' He looked around the group. 'Well, when shall we three meet again . . . Or *four*,' he added, with what seemed to Hooper like a remarkably scathing glance at him.

'I'll ring you tomorrow,' Scruby said.

'Right.'

'What *happened*?' Hooper asked Roger urgently.

Roger said nothing for a moment. Then only, 'I'll tell you later.' He looked at Mark Varda. 'Thank you,' he mumbled.

'Not at all,' the barrister beamed. 'My pleasure.' He gave a quick wave of his hand and was gone.

The others moved towards the exit at a slower pace.

'Now you do appreciate,' Leonard Scruby spoke to Roger, 'that this is only the first hurdle? We have to come back here in a week's time and before that we'll have to meet with Mr Varda again and make plans.'

Roger nodded. They passed out of the lobby on to the court-house steps. 'Good,' said Scruby. He unfastened his attaché case and took out a printed form. 'Now the next job is to serve this on your wife and collect the boy . . . Will she be at home?'

Roger looked out at the traffic. 'I know where Richard will be,' he said slowly. 'At playgroup . . . Cheryl'll be coming to collect him at four.'

The solicitor nodded thoughtfully. 'What might be a very good idea,' he said at length, 'would be for you to go and collect your son before she gets there. Then I can serve the order on her when she arrives. That way,' he explained, 'we can avoid any unpleasantness. It can be distressing removing a child in the presence of its parent. Though usually,' he mused, 'they're too shocked to put up much opposition. Still . . . it would be better if we could do it without fuss.'

Roger nodded. As they waited to sight a taxi, Scruby spoke again suddenly. 'There's a problem.' The others looked at him. 'If you've gone away with your boy, Mr Miles . . . well, I don't know what your wife looks like.'

'I do,' said Hooper.

Scruby glanced at him. 'Ah . . . ' He nodded. 'Then there's no problem.'

Mark Varda must have found a taxi straight away for

there was no sign of him, but it took them ten minutes before they could stop a vacant one. 'We may not get there in time,' Scruby fretted as they moved off into traffic that was beginning to grow towards rush-hour proportions. 'In which case, Mr Miles – brace yourself!'

But they were lucky. They got to Richard's playgroup, held in a church hall just off Acre Lane, with minutes to spare. Scruby and Hooper sat in the taxi as Roger went into the hall, and then soon after reappeared hand-in-hand with Richard who was well bundled-up against the weather. Roger waved towards the taxi, and then father and son set off up the street towards the bus-stop on the main road.

'We going to be waiting long?' said the taxi-driver.

'No. Not long,' said Scruby. He gazed out of the window at the houses, the church hall, the forlorn bare trees. 'Depressing area,' he commented at last. 'Do you know it at all?'

'Quite well,' said Hooper. 'I used to live near here.'

'Ah . . . I live near Ascot,' Scruby remarked thankfully.

The taxi-meter clicked on another notch. The driver yawned and settled deeper into his seat. Scruby fidgeted beside Hooper, who wondered if the lawyer was uneasy about what he would soon have to do. But perhaps it was only the awkwardness of the two of them sitting here, side by side in silence.

'Do *you* have any children, Mr Hooper?' Scruby came up with eventually.

'Little boy.'

'Ah. What age?'

'Four.'

'Nice age. They're very nice, boys at that age. Four, five, six, eight, ten . . . anything up to twelve, in fact.' After a moment, he added, 'I have a boy.'

Hooper nodded. He knew. He remembered the conversation about 'Neville' and the boat to Barbados. 'How old is he?'

'Thirteen,' said Scruby gloomily.

At that moment, looking out of the window, Hooper saw a splash of colour in the general grey. Cheryl Langford, in a glowing pink track-suit, was cycling up the street. She stopped her bike outside the church hall, and exchanged a few laughing words with a couple of other mothers.

'That's her,' he said, pointing.

Leonard Scruby stepped swiftly out of the taxi. But before he could cross the road, Cheryl had already gone into the hall. Hooper watched as the solicitor took up a position outside the door. In a little while the woman reappeared. He could see, with a twinge of amusement, that her expression was very puzzled. Scruby stepped forward and said something to her. When she nodded, he opened his brief-case and took out the form. He handed it to her, speaking again. She took the form but did not look at it; instead she stared into the solicitor's face. Scruby said something more. And then turned from her and crossed the road again. He climbed into the taxi.

'Bond Street tube,' he instructed the driver in an even tone. And then, as the taxi moved off, 'Can I drop you anywhere?' he enquired of Hooper in the same temperate manner.

Hooper was craning his neck to watch Cheryl Langford out of the back window. Really he wished they could have waited a bit longer outside the church hall. He felt he hadn't seen nearly enough. Only when she had entirely passed from his vision, when the boastful pink of her costume had faded altogether into the gloom, did he turn round and answer the solicitor's question.

'Bond Street will do fine,' he said.

17

The next few days passed very happily for Hooper. He saw nothing of Roger Miles, though he spoke to him on the phone a couple of times. He was not living at his house. On the evening of the day he had gained possession of his son, his wife had shown up demanding to be let in. When he had refused, Cheryl had spent the next hour shrieking and cursing wildly in the road outside. In the end, the neighbours had called the police who had finally persuaded her to come away. The little boy had been disturbed to hear his mother's screams –

'Well, he was bound to be,' said Hooper.

– and to prevent a recurrence of the incident, Roger had taken him to stay at a friend's flat, north of the river. He was pretty sure Cheryl did not know the address. He had heard that she had been ringing round all their friends, desperate to find out where her son had been taken. It was mostly a shame, he told Hooper, that he could not risk taking Richard to his playgroup. The little boy was getting bored with no companions. Time dragged a bit, with just the two of them.

'But you're not sorry you did it?' Hooper asked anxiously.

'Of course not!' came Roger's voice, strong and confident.

'I thought you seemed a bit quiet the other day. Towards the end.'

'Well, I think it just happened so fast, that's all,' said Roger.

'Yes,' Hooper agreed. 'It did.'

Roger had had a couple of sessions with Leonard Scruby and one with Varda and he was hopeful about the outcome of the hearing fixed for the following Wednesday. Before they hung up, he asked Hooper to come along to court.

'But I'm not allowed in.'

'I'd still like you to be around.'

So Hooper agreed, and hung up, pleased that things were working out so well in his friend's life.

In his own life too he had found a sudden surge of promise. Mysteriously a barrier seemed to have melted between himself and Emmy. He had gone over to her flat as usual on Saturday at noon to collect Christopher. She had taken him swimming that morning at the Manor Baths and her curly hair was still damp. They didn't exchange more than the customary couple of bare sentences about what time he would be bringing Christopher back. But out on the Common he found himself remembering with affection Emmy's prowess as a swimmer. Though small and seemingly delicate, in the water she was powerful and tireless. It was a good job for him that she was. There was a possibility that she had saved his life once. Years ago, before Christopher was born, they had gone camping to Yugoslavia. One evening they had set off to swim the few hundred yards from one headland to the next. Half-way across he had begun to struggle. His arms and legs had turned heavy and weak. He was too embarrassed at first to call out. But he had started to swallow water and, however hard he kicked, his legs seemed to drift obstinately downward, towing his body beneath the sea.

It was dark now, stars and moon sharp in the sky. The land seemed so close. On the beach between the headlands a party of German tourists had built a bonfire and were sporting round it, loud and energetic. He could see their faces, but he knew he could not make it to the shore where they played. He turned himself around and tried to struggle back the way he had come. He made no progress in that direction either. The cold was seeping into him, and with it at last the notion that he was in danger. He yelled for Emmy. She turned in the water, fifty yards ahead, and saw his trouble. She swam swiftly back to him and got him to turn over on his back. Then she worked herself under his body and, with one arm across his chest, back-stroked them to safety with her free arm. The last few yards he broke away from her and swam unaided and competently to the shore.

'Well, you look all right,' she complained when she joined him.

'I am,' he said. 'Just got a bit panicky for a moment.'

They didn't talk about it much at the time. Sometimes over the years he thought back to the incident and wondered if he had truly been in danger. Even if he had, no doubt one of the Germans would have been only too glad to plunge in and pull him out. He was unwilling to believe anything so definite as that he owed his life to Emmy – though he could remember well how he had rested against her breast with such relief as she towed him through the sea. When he asked her, she couldn't quite remember all the circumstances of the rescue either. It became part of the affectionate, comic side of their life together, the best part – the night Emmy had 'saved him from drowning'.

The afternoon with Christopher passed happily, even though they were not able this Saturday to go to Roger Miles's house. Hooper had taken the trouble to research other possibilities, and had noticed that there was a play for children on at the Arts Centre at half-past two. So after their ramble round the Common, and after lunch at McDonald's, they walked up Lavender Hill to the Centre. There were about thirty children in the theatre, interspersed with a scattering of parents – among them, he noted, a preponderance of lone fathers. The piece was presented by a group called Concealed Weapons Theatre Company. The Dragon Thatcher sits guarding half a dozen pots of gold, with the aid of Inspector Cruelty and Colonel Blunderbuss. Against these are ranged an heroic quintet composed of one skinhead, one Rastafarian, one single parent, a member of the unemployed, and a large, eager girl in the role of Britannia. The play was full of incident and performed with hectic enthusiasm. The dragon, the policeman and the soldier were killed many times before their final, permanent decease, when their conquerors sat, feet resting on the carcasses, leading their excited audience through a medley of songs that began in the dim past with 'We Shall Overcome', continued rousingly through 'Give Peace a Chance' and 'Yellow Submarine', and at last swooped forward to a defiant anthem of the present time:

We don't need no education,
We don't need no thought control.
No dark sarcasm in the classroom,
Teacher leave them kids alone . . .

All in all, you're just a –
Nother brick in the wall.

Hooper, a veteran of agit-prop – who once, impersonating General Westmoreland, had driven a cardboard tank through Grosvenor Square – was not hostile to this scenario, but he wasn't much held by it either. What caught his attention from the beginning was the girl playing the part of Britannia. She was big and ungainly and pale, and there was an air about her that spoke of many disappointments, of frequent, heavy periods, and of social embarrassments without number. Yet there she was, throwing herself into the part with tearing abandon, her eyes sparking with excitement as she crashed around the tiny stage. He marvelled, and he felt humble before this creature who, with the odds against her and every reason to whimper her way through life, had had the courage to choose a path that led to happiness for her. He hoped it would not fail her for a long time. He thought there was a lesson for himself in her gallantry. And when at the end she faced the audience, breasts heaving and bits of tin-foil armour dropping off her in showers, and cried out 'Wasn't that *super*?', he was on his feet with the rest, cheering his assent.

18

They went back to Emmy's flat exhilarated from the play, and they must have looked very cheerful when she opened the door for she took the risk of asking Hooper in once more for a cup of tea. And he found himself actually nodding and stepping into the apartment – the first time he had been inside for many months.

While Christopher went to the living-room and the TV set, Hooper nervously followed his wife into the kitchen. 'I take it *he's* not around.'

Emmy sighed as she placed the kettle on the gas ring.

'He's not around,' she said. 'He's never around.'

He stared at her. 'Well, he lives here, doesn't he?'

'No. He doesn't.'

After a moment, he asked in a small voice, 'Since when?'

'A month ago.'

' . . . Why didn't you tell me?'

'Oh *Bill*,' she sighed. 'You won't let me say a word.'

He sat down heavily at the kitchen table. 'Do you still see him?'

She shrugged. 'I've seen him a couple of times. But there's nothing any more. There never was much. But I was lonely . . . I'd been lonely for so long after you left.'

'And you're not now?'

'Yes . . . But I'm all right. We do OK on our own.'

'We?'

'Your son and me.'

When he was stirring his tea, he said, 'Are you angry with me? I didn't make it very easy for you with him.'

'No, you didn't,' she agreed. 'You were a sod.'

He looked up, and to his relief saw she was smiling slightly. Could all this become one of their affectionate memories too? He chuckled. 'When I scratched out 'I'll kill you" on the front door . . . ' he reminded her.

Her smile dropped away. 'That wasn't at all funny,' she warned. 'I had to pay the porter to get that taken off.'

He grew solemn too. 'How much?'

'Ten quid.'

He got it out of his wallet and handed it over. 'Do you need any more?'

She shook her head.

'I've got lots,' he urged.

'Oh . . . OK,' she nodded, somewhat to Hooper's surprise. But he gave her everything he had on him – about forty pounds – and she tucked it away efficiently in the table drawer.

'How could I not have known he'd gone?' he mused as he started on his second cup of tea.

'Because you're so shut off. You don't talk to anybody.'

He nodded. 'It's true.' He watched her. 'What else have I missed? What's going on?'

'Alice and Sean have broken up.'

'No kidding,' he marvelled. 'Mind you,' he added sagely, 'there were strains.'

'His drinking.'

'Her personality.' He stopped. 'Go on. What else?'

'Did you hear about Amy?'

'Amy Dunn?' He shook his head. 'I haven't seen her since . . . ' Since that lunch at the Steins', he remembered suddenly. 'What's happened to Amy?'

'She got stabbed.'

'Christ! Where?'

'In Grafton Square.'

'But *where*? On her?'

'In her back . . . She was walking home. Two boys came up behind her and pushed her down and grabbed her bag. She didn't know they'd done anything else to her till she got home. She was furious about losing the money and her bank cards and everything. And then somebody in the house noticed there was blood all over the back of her coat . . . She says at least she stopped worrying about the money after that.

'But *stabbed* . . . Was it bad?'

'She was in hospital for a couple of days. She's all right

now . . . The worst of it, she says, is just to know they could have killed her and they didn't care. They didn't need to do it to get her bag away. They just wanted to do it.'

'That's awful.' Hooper scowled. Then sighed. 'Poor Amy . . . I should go and see her.'

'You should.'

'Stabbed!' He shook his head and looked at his wife. 'Do you think this neighbourhood's had it? Maybe we should move?'

She stared at him then.

'I mean,' he explained carefully, 'that you and Chris should move.'

'But where could we go?'

It was not an easy one. 'Putney?' he hazarded.

'Dulwich?' wondered Emmy.

In the end, none of the South London localities that they mentioned particularly appealed. It did not occur to either to suggest anywhere north of the river. Like most people who had lived in the south for any length of time, they had certain rooted prejudices. Such as that the mean annual temperature of North London was at least five degrees cooler. And that the region was populated exclusively by gangsters, rich foreigners, and provincials on the make. Moreover, they felt towards their own side of the Thames a sort of protective affection as towards a slightly deformed or backward child. They knew their part of London was regarded as a bit of a joke elsewhere in the capital. They knew the gags about 'transpontines' and that it was supposed to be funny to say 'garridge'. They were determined not to be ashamed.

'We'd be mad to leave the Common,' Emmy urged. 'It's a desirable area. Everybody says so.'

'Bit of luck for Amy. It it wasn't, she might have got really hurt.'

'All right. But think about it. It's nice here. The schools are good. And there's fresh air. And it's close to everything . . . We couldn't leave the Common.'

'I suppose not,' he sighed. He remembered something then, and found he wanted to tell it to her. 'D'you know, I just found out my mother grew up round here.'

'I thought she came from Hampshire.'

'So did I. But last time I was down there she told me she was born in Cedars Road. Didn't leave the Common till she was five. I never knew it. And now, look, we've landed up here . . . Well, you have,' he corrected himself. 'And I will soon,' he added. She looked at him curiously. 'I've decided to get a flat,' he told her. 'This hotel business is ridiculous.'

'When did you decide that?'

'Recently.' In fact about thirty seconds ago. 'I want somewhere I can take Christopher to,' he said. 'And . . . maybe he could stay over one night a week? . . . two nights? . . . if you wouldn't mind.'

'That's what I *want*,' she sighed. 'That's what I wanted to talk to you about.'

So they talked and made plans, and a half-hour passed very pleasantly – except for one flare-up. That was when she had got up to make more tea. She pushed a newspaper across the table to him and pointed to a story. 'Isn't that dreadful?' she said.

It was much worse than that. It was an account from Scotland of some sort of orgy or gang-bang – three youths were involved and a woman much older than they. One of the boys had been drunk and had failed to get an erection. Mortified, he had pulled out a cut-throat razor and slashed the woman with it over and over about her face and breasts and vagina. Hooper read all this with a sort of sickly fascination. The brutal images excited his imagination. He seemed to see so clearly the damp and dark and cold, the filthy shed, the stink of sex and cheap wine, and the cruel little thug in his humiliation, and then the poor woman's terror and pain. The blood . . . He shoved the paper away from him. 'Good Lord!' he cried out. 'Why are you showing me this?'

'Why – !' Her eyes opened innocently wide. 'Why I just thought you'd be interested.'

'Interested.'

'After Amy and everything.'

But that bad moment passed. Soon he was able to take up the paper again and, turning quickly over the page that carried the Scottish horror-story, to check the Flats for Sale columns to see what prices were like these days.

'I should think you'd do better at an estate agent,' Emmy said, watching him fondly over the rim of her cup.

They finished their tea at last. Then she asked him to stay for supper. He said he couldn't. She asked him if he had somewhere to go, and he shook his head. He hadn't. Not really.

'But I don't feel I can sit down and eat with you. Not yet.'

They went out of the kitchen into the hall, and there they found Christopher sitting cross-legged, leaning against the wall. Hooper stopped laughing beside his son.

'What are you doing down there?'

'Listening!' cried the little boy happily.

Emmy sent him to lay the table for their supper and accompanied her husband to the front door. He said, not looking at her, 'Well, I did enjoy it . . . talking.' He stopped. It was difficult for him to say the next thing. But he got to it. 'I wish I could have done it before I knew . . . the other person . . . he'd gone.'

Emmy nodded. 'I wish you could have too,' she stated.

It irritated him that she seemed not to acknowledge that it had been a hard thing for him to say. 'Well, fuck it,' he snapped. 'I'm only human . . . "My other daddy",' he quoted accusingly at her.

On this new spasm of anger they parted. But in the car he found he was feeling very content. He parked at the Junction end of Lavender Hill and got out and looked in the windows of several estate agents. There seemed to be a good selection on offer, and prices weren't as high as he'd been expecting. He noted down several possibilities, planning to ring about them on Monday morning. Then in the car, all the way back to Hammersmith, he thought of Emmy. One particular image, like ten seconds of black and white TV, kept playing through his mind. It was not long after they had met at university. She was sixteen, an infant prodigy up from Somerset, tiny, dainty, fizzing with life. Almost the first thing he had noticed about her was that if he touched the top of her head, the scalp through her fine hair felt burning hot. This became a phenomenon on campus. People – until Emmy got bored with it – almost queued up to touch her head. It was generally supposed that the heat was generated by the furious mental activity taking place within her skull. For she was the *wunderkind*, Kid Calculus: rumours of her impending arrival had been sweeping the maths department for a year before she showed up.

('I could have had anyone at university,' she used to complain to him with increasing seriousness over the years. 'And I took *you*!')

The weekend after they had first slept together, they had a date to meet in London. On a cold, sleety day he had approached the Tate Gallery, ten minutes early for their meeting. She was already there, waiting on the top of the steps. She darted towards him, hair flying, dancing down the steps. They had gone into each other's arms; and then, automatically, he had brought one hand up to rest on her scalp. He had no gloves and his hands were freezing. Gratefully he warmed first one and then the other against the steady glow from her head.

And this scene he now played over and over as he drove across Wandsworth Bridge and then threaded his way through the back streets to the New Kings Road. The young girl flying down the steps. It blotted out all the other later images from the times after he had graduated and Emmy, to her professors' fury, had dropped out of college to marry him and go with him on their long, meandering travels abroad. Emmy resentful, Emmy tearful, angry, aggrieved. And at last Emmy ageing, Emmy adulterous . . . And then the hate, then the smash. Over it all pattered the image of the young girl, 'He has something you can never have . . . He knew me when I was nineteen.' Sixteen! The light of that knowledge still incredibly glimmered for him through the years. Even when he hated her, if he heard her name suddenly, or thought of it himself, he would start to smile. He could not control it.

19

The warm feelings of Saturday carried him over the rest of the weekend and accompanied him to work on Monday. He was astonished at the reactions he got in the office. People greeted him as if he'd just returned from a six-month trip abroad. It awed him to think how badly he must have behaved over the past few months to be getting such a response now, for all he was doing was just smiling and chatting perfectly normally.

'You look *great*, Bill,' people kept saying to him as he moved in sprightly style around the building.

'Well, thanks, I feel pretty good,' he'd reply complacently.

The only one who seemed resistant to his new-found charms was his closest, dearest colleague, Creighton Phillips. In fact, the advertising manager behaved most coolly towards him, though Hooper favoured him with some of his best smiles. In the end he cornered Creighton at lunchtime in the pub down the road from the office and asked him what the hell the matter was.

'I know I've been a pain lately,' he confessed. 'But you know I've had troubles . . . '

Creighton nodded. 'Yes,' he said, in a tone that was far from forgiving. 'Yes, you have been a pain.' He looked up from his drink and Hooper was appalled to see real hurt in his old chum's eyes. 'You've been saying some pretty strange things lately, Bill,' Creighton added.

'Look . . .' Hooper drew a stool up to the counter. 'I don't know what I've been saying. I've been half out of my mind, you know that.' And when Creighton didn't respond, he said irritably, 'All right. What's the terrible thing I've said?'

'You said,' Creighton enunciated, 'that I belong in an alcoholic ward and that you should be flogged.'

Hooper stared. 'I said *I* should be flogged?'

'And I belong in an alcoholic ward.'

'*Flogged!* I said that?'

'And me in an alcoholic ward,' Creighton reminded him. 'Do you think that, Bill?' he burst out. 'Do you really?'

Hooper, appealed to, looked guiltily into his friend's anxious eyes. Lord, what fears he must have stirred up in the poor man. 'Well, you do drink quite a lot, Creighton . . .' he started uncertainly.

'I've cut it down,' Creighton chipped in eagerly. He looked down at his glass and pushed it away from him a couple of inches. 'Way down.'

They sat side by side. At length Hooper sighed, 'What else did I say?'

Creighton pondered the question, evidently having a selection to choose from. 'You said we were a pair of incompetent fools, you and me,' he stated finally. 'You said we ought to be shipped out to labour camps.'

'Surely not? Labour camps! *Where?*'

'Your very words. You must mean it, Bill,' Creighton went on, as Hooper groaned and held his head. 'Somewhere you must mean it.'

Hooper tried to reply several times. 'It's just,' he said at last, 'I think I've been feeling guilty for a long time.'

'About what?'

'About the work. About Overton's. Us.'

'What have we done?' Creighton demanded. 'We do

our jobs. What have we got to be ashamed of?'

'We're never at risk,' Hooper tried to explain. 'And all these kids on Editorial . . . they come in. If they're lucky they get to work for a year. And if we mess up they're bunged out in a few months . . . It's been weighing on me.'

'But that's not our fault,' said Creighton amazed. 'That's just how it is.'

'I was thinking mostly,' said Hooper gloomily, 'about *Giants*. That was my fault.'

Giants had been a scheme entirely devised by Hooper some years back, in his capacity as an originator of bright new ideas, whereby magazine-length biographies were commissioned of fairly-old famous people and set in type so that they could be stock-piled against the day of the person's death when they would be brought out, printed up, and distributed to bookshops and newsagents, almost – as Hooper had mordantly quipped in his presentation – before the body was cold. Hooper had received many compliments from the directors for this scheme and a gratifying increase in salary. In fact, when it finally came into operation, sales of the first two post-humous biographies were disappointingly small and the whole project was then cancelled. But it could be argued that that was the fault of blind chance that had made Lyndon Johnson and Cecil Day Lewis the subject of the first two biographies for, in their separate ways, they were probably the weakest candidates on Hooper's list from a sales point of view. And in the end few criticisms descended on Hooper's head. It was agreed that it had been a bold and interesting experiment, and besides he was by then deeply involved in another promising project, which, as it happened, turned out very profitably. The youthful editorial staff of *Giants* all had to be let go, however.

'It wasn't your fault,' Creighton argued. 'Blame C. Day Lewis for not writing better poetry. If Auden had died six months earlier it might have been a whole different story.'

Hooper shook his head firmly, the professional rising in

him too. 'No, no. You'd have needed a really big death to get that one off the ground. De Gaulle. Churchill. Presley . . . And even then it was probably a no-hope idea. Mine,' he sorrowed.

'It was a bold and interesting experiment,' Creighton urged.

'It was a pathetic disaster and a lot of people lost their jobs,' Hooper said angrily. 'But not me. Never me.'

Creighton too was suddenly angry. 'Why are you knocking yourself, Bill?' he demanded. 'You're good at your job. You work like hell. Some of the time. Think of all the successes you've had.'

'Think of all the flops,' said Hooper. 'And who paid for them.'

He had started slowly to get to his feet, when Creighton reached out suddenly to seize his arm. 'What shall we do about it?'

'What?'

'For the kids. You're right. They deserve a better deal. What'll we do? Go to the directors? Resign? I'm with you, Bill. Tell you what,' Creighton beamed. 'Next time they try and start a union here, we'll join, shall we? Shall we? Whatever you say, Bill.'

Hooper gazed at his old friend. Creighton's veined face was alive and bold, his bloodshot eyes bright with valour. The poor man, Hooper thought. With all his debts and his boozing and his mortgage and his marriages and his family. And here he was, for a couple of minutes at least, offering to risk all he had – his job, in fact. He realised suddenly that this was another cursed with afflicting memories of old British movies. He could not quite place this one, though he knew he had seen it. Creighton was playing the silly ass who reveals at last he has a heart of gold and will follow his captain anywhere, yea into the jaws of death if need be.

And he, Hooper, was supposed to be the captain. If it wasn't sad, it was funny. He signalled for the barman to bring Creighton another drink.

'We can't join a union,' he explained. 'We're management . . . No, there's nothing to be done,' he said (though dimly aware that he had not given it much thought). 'Except I don't plan to be what I used to be any more.'

'What do you mean?' said Creighton, reaching for his new drink.

'I'm going to keep my mouth shut,' Hooper vowed. 'Not so many jokes. Not so much the acid wit. I'm tired of being a clever young man. I'm not God's gift to anybody, Creighton, and it's time I started to act like it.' After a moment, 'Quite clever,' he amended himself with determined honesty. 'Not really young.'

'Come on! Look at you. Still not a grey hair on your head. Or only four or five.'

'That's true,' Hooper brightened. Then he scowled. 'But it's not the point either . . . I've got to fucking well *change*. That's the point.'

'Now hang on,' Creighton protested. 'You weren't so bad, Bill. We had a few laughs, you must admit.'

Hooper shook his head. 'I'm going to be different,' he insisted.

Creighton mumbled something into his glass.

'What's that?'

'I said,' Creighton stated more clearly, 'I shall be lonely.'

20

What kept Hooper particularly buoyed up in this time, of course, was his cheerful anticipation of the next round of Roger Miles's custody battle. He phoned his friend on Tuesday evening to wish him well. Roger had moved back into the house with his son. He sounded cautiously optimistic.

'I was thinking,' Hooper said. 'Instead of going to court, shall I look after Richard? I'd be happy to do it.'

'No, thanks. That's under control.'

'How is he?'

'Richard? He's fine.'

'So . . . ' There was a silence between them. 'Nothing to report?'

'Not really.'

'Well, no news is . . . and so on,' Hooper laughed self-consciously. 'Well, good luck. Or break a leg. Or – '

'We've been working on the Evidences,' Roger said, with a touch of insider's swank.

After a moment, Hooper conceded, 'All right. What are they?'

'The things we'll be saying against Cheryl. We have to put them all together. Inform the other side.'

'I thought you'd done all that? The affidavit.'

'Well, this is some other stuff. I've been kept quite busy. Varda's been over to help. He's just left.'

'That's not usual is it – coming over?' Hooper felt strangely jealous.

'Well, I think it's something personal,' Roger said.

'In what way?'

'He wants to win.'

Just before they hung up, Roger said suddenly, 'You know Cheryl's got Jane Powell acting for her?'

'Ah . . . ' Hooper thought about this. 'Well, she's supposed to be good . . . But I think Varda's pretty good too. Don't you?'

'Oh, yes. I was just thinking . . . she's a friend of yours, isn't she?'

'That's neither here nor there,' Hooper told him firmly. 'See you tomorrow.'

But after he'd hung up, he couldn't help wondering at the fate that had brought him and Janey Powell into opposing camps. For it was true, they had been close once. Sometimes when he was driving along the Fulham Palace Road and other streets in West London he caught glimpses of an old slogan scribbled in white emulsion on walls and the ends of terraces: FREE OZ. This was the handiwork of Janey Powell. She had wielded the brush, Hooper had held the paint-tin. For a little while they had been assisted by a mutual friend, Tony Herring, who they had met in the street as they set out on this expedition. But Tony had tickets to a Cream concert, and had had to leave early.

When he saw those words now, chipped and faded as they had become, Hooper sometimes mused on how, for many people well into adult life, they must have the remote mysterious quality of Egyptian hieroglyphics. The suppression of the old flower-power magazine, the arrest and trial of its editors – all was buried under the years and the weight of much worse wrongs and much angrier responses. (A couple of years after the painting expedition, Tony Herring had been picked up by the Bomb Squad, accused of being part of a group that planned to dynamite Army Recruiting Centres to protest against the Bloody Sunday massacre in Ireland. The whole thing had been a disaster. Half the group turned out to be informers, and they had only been able to get hold of some railway detonators anyway. Tony had got eighteen months in prison.)

Still in its day the *Oz* affair had seemed scandal enough to send Jane Powell – no fool, then or now – out into the streets with a burning anger in her breast, a pot of paint left over from the new flat at Putney Bridge she was painting, and Hooper dragging along behind her as a reluctant accomplice. He would have preferred to stay in the flat and listen to some music. And, as a matter of fact, to go to bed with Janey. They had never come so close to it before that day and never were to come so close again. But she, adamant, had hustled him out into the street.

On that evening, years ago, Janey was wearing the canary-yellow straw Stetson hat she had brought back from Cuba, a schoolboy's striped blazer, a mauve miniskirt, white net stockings and a pair of crimson sandals bound to her feet by leather thongs that reached up to her knees. They had been smoking grass all afternoon and were alternately paranoically nervous and hysterically mirthful. People peered out at them from passing cars as they painted away. At one point Janey got so overcome she pissed herself and sat on the pavement, the puddle spreading out from beneath her, her shoulders heaving with laughter. But he had never doubted the sincerity of her anger. It was all part of it then: anger and laughter and dope and music and the funny clothes.

Nowadays, Hooper knew Jane Powell did not care to look back fondly on such faraway escapades. She was far too busy, for one thing. In addition to all the time she put in at the law centre, she had been sitting for several years now on her local council. She had spent most of her evenings in this time wrangling with the neanderthal, largely Irish leadership of her own party – most of whom had lately gone over to the Social Democrats which may have made her life a little easier. A year to two back a newspaper – in order to ridicule the level of debate in that particular council – had published a portion of the previous night's transcript. Hooper had cut it out and had kept the clipping in his wallet. It read in part:

COUNCILLOR POWELL: Mr Chairperson –
COUN. ROURKE: Sit down. You are a bitter and confused woman.
COUN. POWELL: Mr Chairperson, I demand the right –
COUN. MICHAELSON: Somebody keep that slag quiet.
COUN. POWELL: Shut up!
COUN. KELLEY: Mr Chairman, if Councillor Powell wishes for the name and address of a reliable marriage bureau, I would be only too happy to oblige her.
COUN. POWELL: —— you!
COUNCILLORS: Order! Order!

Ah Janey . . . She took papers home from the various committees she served on and worked on them far into the night. She suffered from headaches all the time and her face now was usually clenched and tense with pain. Nobody was sure any more what her sex life consisted of, but it was rumoured that she sometimes went into pubs and picked up very young men for one-night stands. She had lately, in addition to everything else, got very deeply involved in the nuclear disarmament campaign and she had frightening secret information about the number of times the Americans had moved by mistake into a nuclear alert. Hooper had so much admiration for her and her dedication and hard work. 'I have nothing but respect for Jane Powell,' he had said often over the years whenever her case came up for discussion around dinner-tables or at parties. Particularly did he feel this when he reflected on his own static uselessness. But other thoughts about her often pressed up inside him too, and if he dared he would say out loud: she has become a bore, a drudge, she is less than she was. And sometimes he thought she had become half-crazy.

He did once, a year or so back, try to suggest to Janey that the way she was carrying on might be costing her a lot.

'I don't know why it is, Bill,' she had said after a few moments thought.

'Why what is?'

'Why you make such a song and dance about it. Just go ahead and admit it. You'll feel better.'

'Admit what?'

'That you've lost your faith,' she had said, with oldtime simplicity.

Brooding over all this in bed that night in the Sandringham, Hooper found himself thinking of the third member of that *Free Oz* painting expedition. Tony Herring had come out of jail and been lavishly received by all his friends. Then he seemed to disappear, and the next thing Hooper heard was that he was out in India and there were scandalised whispers that he had 'gone religious'. He returned one summer with a new Indian name and a wispy beard, dressed in an orange gown, with orange socks and plimsolls. None of the friends could take him seriously. Soon he disappeared again.

Hooper wondered sadly what had ever become of him. Nobody talked about him, he hadn't heard his name mentioned in years. He remembered the orange socks especially, and the way Tony's skinny, hairless legs had appeared touchingly whenever he sat down and hitched up his orange dress.

21

Wednesday dawned cold and grey, but the weather did not affect Hooper's spirits. He had to go into the office in the morning, but had arranged time off after lunch. The hearing was scheduled for 2.30 and he was in the courthouse by 2.15. Roger Miles was already in the lobby. There was no sign of Varda and Leonard Scruby.

Roger introduced him to the elderly man standing at his side. His father. He was a small, meek-looking man, so slight of stature that Hooper presumed straight away that Roger must have got his bulk and strength from his mother who, he gathered, was back at the house looking after Richard. Mr Miles senior looked up at Hooper in a startled, accusing way when they shook hands, as though he suspected him of being at the bottom of this whole mess. Roger stressed that Hooper was his friend, but the old man continued to regard him very thoughtfully as they stood there, waiting and silent.

After ten minutes the lawyers joined them.

'Sorry, we've been put off,' Scruby announced.

'Put off?' repeated Roger.

'Till 3.15.'

Mark Varda looked around the lobby. 'Any sign of the

opposition?' he asked. He chuckled then in a gleeful way. 'I'm so glad it's Jane Powell we're up against.'

'Opponent worthy of your steel?' Hooper asked. It was not a good remark to make, though in a way he meant it genuinely. But of course it came out sounding like a sneer, one of those sneers he had been so adept at once, before he had changed. But Varda could not know about this transformation. He looked at Hooper, quick and angry, and then turned abruptly to Scruby.

'I don't actually think she's got much of a chance though, do you, Leonard?'

Before Scruby could answer, Roger said, 'I thought she was a solicitor.'

'She is.'

'I thought they weren't allowed to speak in court.'

'In a county court, it's perfectly all right,' Scruby explained.

'In fact,' nodded Varda, 'she's an excellent advocate. I've heard her. Really, if anyone could pull this off, it'd be Janey.'

They had forty minutes to kill, and Varda suggested a stroll. Roger's father preferred to wait on a bench and Scruby, wanting to look through some papers on another case, also elected to stay behind. The others wandered around in the little streets behind the Junction. They were overflowing with rubbish. At several points they had to step off the pavement on to the road to avoid the piles of ordure.

'Ah, South London,' breathed Mark Varda. 'It has a flavour all its own, doesn't it?' And then, unexpectedly, he started to move his polished shoes through the filth in a passable imitation of a soft-shoe shuffle, at the same time singing in a light tenor voice:

Wading through the muck and mire,
'Hello, Muck! Hiya, Meyer!'

'Incidentally,' he added, 'just remembered: some people I know who live down here were burgled the other day.

Two boys about twelve, thirteen. One of them was carrying a sawn-off shotgun. I mean!'

'Where was this?' Hooper asked quickly.

'Balham.'

'That's *miles* away. You might as well say,' Hooper scoffed, 'that you should move out of Holland Park because there's been a hold-up in Shepherd's Bush.'

'I wasn't suggesting anybody should *move*,' said the barrister mildly, but not looking at all at Hooper. 'Merely an item of interest.'

As they clambered over piles of garbage to enter another street, Roger informed them, somewhat unnecessarily, that the dustmen were in dispute with the local council.

Mark Varda nodded. 'The awkward squad!' he murmured.

The so-dated phrase irritated Hooper greatly. Like an old, tired limb, his brain creaked towards the proper response to this. 'I suppose *you* think they should take a cut in pay,' he snapped at last.

'Not at all,' said the barrister coldly. 'As a matter of fact, I think they should be paid twice as much. And that there should be about two-thirds fewer of them employed . . . It always comes back to the question of surplus people,' he murmured. 'Doesn't it? Where does one put them all? In the old days there was . . . America . . . Australia . . . ' He lowered his head as if in mourning for all the vanished dumping grounds.

'Actually,' said Roger, 'it's not about pay. The council wants to put the job out to a private firm.'

'Ah, excellent!' gleamed Varda. 'Isn't this a time to live!' he cried. 'To feel the ice breaking? Change in the air? Doesn't really matter how it changes, does it? As long as it does!'

Hooper opened his mouth to object strenuously to all this, but the lawyer, seeing him about to speak, struck first. 'But change would be the last thing *you'd* want, I suppose?'

'Absolutely untrue!' Hooper was shocked by the particularly unjust nature of the accusation. 'Why should you say that?'

'Aren't you a member of the Forever Young generation?' Varda enquired mildly. 'Illusions all intact?'

Hooper, even as he fumed, was puzzled at the amount of hostility crackling between himself and the lawyer. 'Believe me,' he snapped, 'I have no illusions left. None at all!'

Looking across at the lawyer, he thought how good it would be to grab the neat knot of his grey tie and squeeze his throat very tight. At the same time he felt sad it had come to this. For he felt oddly drawn to Varda, in spite of his obnoxiousness, and would have liked to have stood well in the barrister's eyes.

Varda was drawing breath for another riposte when, unexpectedly, Roger spoke up. 'I don't see any harm in illusions,' he said wistfully. And perhaps because it was his policy not to quarrel with clients, Varda swallowed whatever it was he had to say, and they made their way back through the rubbish to the main road in an edgy silence.

As they walked up the hill towards the court-house, they met Scruby who had stepped out for a breath of air. 'The other side has arrived,' he informed them. Hooper glanced at Roger, winked at him encouragingly. He felt a bubble of excitement beginning in his stomach. Varda, as they neared the court, went into his by-now familiar routine, encouraging himself, 'I don't really see what Janey can do, given the Evidences. What do you think, Leonard?' And then, before Scruby could answer, 'Yes, I think we'll have given her something to think about,' Varda chuckled. 'Poor love!'

The hearing was to be held in the court-room itself, not in the judge's private office. As their party approached, people were being cleared from the court, and a woman in a black gown came out and placed a sign outside the door which informed that the forthcoming session was to be held in camera. Reminded, Hooper had started to turn away to join Roger's father on his bench, when Varda looked over at him. 'Seems a shame to miss the fun,' he commented drily. 'When you're obviously so interested. Why don't you come in?'

'I thought I wasn't allowed.'

'Oh, anyone can go in if they've got an excuse.' Varda looked at Scruby. 'Can you use an unpaid clerk for the day, Leonard?'

The solicitor looked at Hooper without much enthusiasm. Eventually he nodded. 'Sit next to me,' he advised. 'Don't say a word. Bow to the judge when you go in and when you leave.'

Hooper had visited a number of court-rooms back when he was helping to prepare Overton's *It's the Law!* legal part-work. He had generally found them to be bustling, human places, with their ever-changing population of policemen and prisoners and lawyers and spectators. But Judge Kirby-Smith's court that afternoon seemed a lonely place. The room had been drably modernised. The walls were off-white, the wood of the tables and chairs brassily veneered. Looking up, he found that the ceiling was divided into fretworked squares. He could see no lamps up there – from a hidden source diffuse light fell impartially on those below. There were no windows. The only patch of colour in the room was where, behind the judge's chair, a dark-blue drape hung, ceiling to floor, backing the royal seal.

Varda and Jane Powell sat in the front row of seats, about a dozen yards apart. Roger, Scruby and Hooper clustered in the second row behind the barrister. Out of the corner of his eye, Hooper could see Cheryl Langford, in a sober, grey coat, sitting alone behind Janey. Her head was bowed, he could not see her expression. He looked up then at the judge. Saw the lean, dark, young-old face, impassive beneath the yellowing pantomime wig. Kirby-Smith was moving around in his high chair, getting himself comfortable, ready to begin.

Hooper's heart beat fast. He forgot the inhospitable surroundings. His moment had arrived. The climax he had yearned for. Moment of justice, vindication . . . *revenge* – and the last word resounded so clearly in his mind it was almost as if he had spoken it out loud.

'Yes, Mr Varda?' he heard the judge say.

22

When it was all over, and Varda and Scruby had left them, and he and Roger were out in the lobby, Hooper offered his congratulations. Then added, 'You weren't exaggerating, were you?'

'What?' said Roger, who was looking around for his father who was no longer sitting on the bench.

'You said you'd been kept busy last week. You must have been.'

'Yes,' said Roger.

Varda had been furnished with the whole catalogue of Cheryl's youthful indiscretions to lay before His Honour. The clashes with the law – for there had been others since the prank with the acid at college. A disorderly conduct conviction following a demonstration in '71. A fine for shop-lifting in '73. A fracas with the authorities in Italy in '74 which had led to her passport being withdrawn for a time. All the way up to the scene outside Roger's home last week when the police had been called to quiet her down.

'Was it like you'd expected?' Hooper asked Roger in the lobby.

'Not really.'

'We've seen too much court-room drama, I suppose.'

'What? Oh – yes . . . I wish I knew where my father's gone.'

'The Gents?' guessed Hooper.

Also on display in the court-room had been the literary evidence of Cheryl's incapacities. A number of small pamphlets had been passed up to the judge's table. Varda had read out certain passages, including the piece Hooper had read in Roger's kitchen. The invitation to violence against men, the enthusiasm for aborting male foetuses, 'female snipers on the rooftop' . . . All of which, Mark Varda had suggested, made their author peculiarly unsuited to the duties of motherhood, particularly where it concerned a small boy.

'I'd almost forgotten that article,' Hooper said to his friend in the lobby. 'It seems ages ago I read it.'

For once Roger looked at him. 'But Janey dealt with that pretty well. Didn't you think?'

'Oh, yes,' Hooper nodded. 'I thought she was very professional.' For it must have cost Jane a little to talk the way she had. All this, she had said, had nothing to do with Mrs Miles's life now. It was all in the past. Mrs Miles had modified her views now. No interest in radical feminism whatsoever . . .

'She kept calling her Mrs Miles,' Roger said wondering. 'I couldn't think who she was talking about for a while.'

As the proceedings wore on, Hooper's sense of disappointment had grown keen. It was his climax – and where was it? It kept slipping away from him. He was hardly able to hear what was going on half the time, everybody muttered so and lost the thread of their arguments and apologised to each other and began again. Jane Powell's brilliance as an advocate, Mark Varda's flair or genius or whatever it was that earned him six hundred pounds a day – well, Hooper couldn't see it. And then there were great gaps while pieces of paper were moved around and passed up to the judge's table. And then more gaps while the judge wrote slowly in the great leather-bound book he had in front of him. Or engaged in whispered conversations with his clerk, the woman in the black gown who had placed the in camera notice outside the court, and who now sat in front of him with a dreamy smile on her face, except when her master claimed her attention. Also Hooper was trying to remember all the time that he himself was supposed to be impersonating some sort of a lawyer and wondering what he ought to be doing and that made him lose track of things very often . . .

Cheryl Langford's lesbianism was the ace in Varda's hand – that much was clear to Hooper at least. Jane Powell kept trying to minimise the damage. Other courts, she reminded the judge, had held recently that a lesbian preference was not an automatic barrier to a woman's ability to be a good mother. And if there was a disadvantage, which she did not wish to concede, did it count solely against the mother in this instance? She put her client into the witness-box. Cheryl, in a low voice, maintained that her sexual relationship with the woman she now lived with had begun even during the period when she had been with Roger, and that he had known of it.

'And what was his attitude to this?'

'He didn't mind . . . I think he quite liked it.'

'Your Honour may well feel,' Jane Powell remarked, when her client had sat down again, 'that if there is a moral stigma attached to this practice, then there is not much difference in guilt between the woman who commits it and the man who permits and – by his attitude – encourages it.'

Mark Varda was quick to put his client in the box in turn. Roger perjured himself adequately.

'You did not then know that your wife was engaging in these practices while you were living with her?'

'No.'

'And what would have been your attitude, do you think, if you had known?'

'I would have been shocked.'

Cheryl Langford suddenly spoke up from where she sat. 'He's lying,' she said in a conversational voice. 'You know you're lying,' she said to Roger.

The judge looked at her crossly. 'Please be quiet,' he said, and she was.

Mark Varda let Roger return to his seat. His client, he informed the judge, wished to provide a normal and natural home background for the child, in contrast to the mother's irregular living arrangements. He intended to keep his job, but as a teacher he had an above-average amount of free time after work and in the holidays to devote to his son. In addition, his parents had agreed to move into his home for four days each week to provide extra care. His client's father was waiting outside if His Honour wished to interview him.

'That won't be necessary, Mr Varda,' said the judge. But he seemed to have listened to the barrister's words with approval, and he made a long note in his book.

Varda wound up his presentation with a glowing tribute to his client's many virtues. His impeccable record at school and university, his steady labours ever since in an honoured profession – in contrast to his wife, who as the barrister mildly pointed out, had never held a job in her life. Hooper lost interest in this speech early on. He was feeling very odd. Very cold inside. At one point while Varda was speaking, he noticed that Jane Powell had turned in her seat and was staring at him. Stupidly, Hooper started to smile at her. Her mouth tightened in a grimace of contempt and she looked away. After that, his gaze shifted to Cheryl Langford who sat with bowed head listening to the praise being heaped upon her husband. She couldn't win, he thought suddenly. Not possibly. And it was as if she knew it. There had been something flat and accepting about her stance all through the proceedings, as she had sat there, as she had listened to the things said against her, and had watched the game uncoil. What chance had she, who had thrown herself into the life of her generation with such abandon, against Roger's inoffensive neutrality? Probably Janey had warned her not to hope too much. For she wouldn't win. Hooper was sure of it.

So it proved. The judge said that he agreed with Miss

Powell to the extent that he would take no notice of the evidence of her client's opinions and writings of ten years before. (Scruby at this point uttered a faint grunt. Hooper, beside him, guessed it was one of scepticism.) On the other hand, His Honour had gained an impression of a woman of considerable instability and rashness. He continued to regard the matter of lesbianism with much seriousness. He appreciated that another court might take a more lenient view, but this was not another court. He confessed himself somewhat unhappy about the question of whether the husband had known of his wife's activities during the time they had lived together. 'I must say . . . ' He peered sternly in Roger's direction, 'that if Mr Miles is not a complaisant husband, then he is at least an extremely unobservant one.'

However, Mr Miles appeared to be a man of excellent character and he would take his word for it. He therefore saw no reason to withdraw the order giving the husband care and control of the child. A lesbian relationship was not the proper setting for the rearing of a child. 'Particularly when it is a boy.' The judge hesitated at this point, perhaps in order to search his mind for a justification for the remark. Apparently nothing presented itself, for His Honour moved on to set a date for the final hearing of the case two months ahead, and ordered a welfare report to be made on both parties.

When he had stopped speaking, Hooper looked across at Cheryl Langford. But not before seeing that everybody else – judge included – was doing just the same. All watched her with a kind of unholy fascination. For a few moments her strong profile was immobile. And then, though she made no sound, tears started to slide from her eyes like a lava flow. Janey reached back and put her arms round her. Hooper glanced at Roger. He was staring glumly at the table-top before him.

The judge stood up, and everyone else followed suit, except for Cheryl who sat and wept. Hooper remembered suddenly how he had cried out 'But that's dishonest!'

when Roger had vowed to lie about his knowledge of her sexual life. He thought he saw now what he had meant. To use her lesbianism against Cheryl was after all only to offend against the customs of their own particular tribe. They were still keeping to the rules of the game, however stupid those rules were. But to conspire to tell lies to get their ends – that was breaking a much older code; it seemed as if they had gone against nature . . .

Yet immediately he formed this explanation, he felt his mind give a shrug of protest and disgust. This cant about the 'rules of the game'. He knew the scene so well. He and Roger were the cowards who had betrayed the tunnel's entrance to the German guards. They were the rats who had run away when the Desert Rats were standing firm. Jack Hawkins was on the bridge and Virginia McKenna was on the shore and they were a pair of snivelling little Richard Attenboroughs down in the coal-hole. It was sickening to be affected by such stuff. He refused to be ashamed.

All the same, out in the lobby he and Roger spoke to each other in very low voices with their eyes averted.

'I wish she hadn't cried,' Roger said, just as they saw his father at last appear, toiling slowly towards them. 'Cheryl never cries.'

They parted like outlaws. On his way back to the hotel, Hooper noticed a slogan freshly-painted on a railway arch: WOMEN SAY NO TO MALE VIOLENCE. Underneath another hand had already mockingly added: YES, DEAR.

Things had not changed, he thought miserably. Would never change. This squabbling and dislike that was consuming them all would never cease. War without end.

23

Hooper's feelings of remorse did not linger long. What right, he was soon fuming, did the woman have to penetrate them with her tears? She had been caught out in the perpetration of a crime, and now by using the age-old device had succeeded in making the innocent parties feel momentarily guilty! Hooper spoke with outrage on this point when he phoned Roger a week or so after the hearing.

'I mean you could cry from here to China and nobody would bat an eyelid. Would they?'

'That's true,' Roger agreed.

'All that happened was that she tried to put one over on us – '

Hooper was not sure he liked Roger's tone of voice. It sounded faintly accusing – but of who or what, he could not tell. He decided to drop the matter. 'Anyway,' he said, 'you feel all right now?'

'Oh, yes.'

'Does this mean you've got Richard for good?'

'Well, there's going to be a final hearing. But Mark says it's virtually certain. He says the beauty of the system is we keep appearing before the same judge. So we get the same result.'

'Yes, that's handy,' Hooper agreed. 'And how's it working out with the parents?'

'Oh . . . few teething-problems. But OK really.'

Hooper waited to hear more, but it was not forthcoming. 'Anyway,' he said at length. 'No regrets?'

'Oh, none at all.'

And they hung up after making a vague arrangement to get together in a week or so's time. Or a couple of weeks. Whenever was convenient.

A major reason for the renewal of Hooper's tough attitude towards Cheryl Langford was the reaction he was getting from several erstwhile good friends. The news of what had been going on – and his own role in it – had had plenty of time to circulate. He might have guessed from the way Jane Powell had looked at him in the court-room that his popularity, which had been shaky for so long, was due for another sharp fall. Still it was a shock to find out how many of the people he encountered over the next few weeks were either cool towards him or actively hostile. Some of them took the trouble to ring him up to tell him of their disapproval, among them Sally Stein who caught him at the office in a meeting with Creighton Phillips.

'You are a vile and despicable bastard!'

'Hello, Sally.'

'Bill, how could you?'

'Are you sure you've got the right number? I wasn't actually a party in this thing, you know.'

'Oh shut up! You know he'd never have done anything on his own. He's far too weak.'

'And now he's strong. Aren't you glad?'

There was a pause, and he listened to her harsh breathing.

'You're not ever coming to my house again,' she gritted at last. 'Sam agrees with me . . . Do you understand? Not ever!'

'That's really devastating news.'

'To use her being gay against her – how can you live with yourself?'

'That was just a tactic,' Hooper said swiftly. Then he prepared himself for his thrust. 'But tell me, Sally — be honest . . . You think she has a right to the kid just because she's a woman. Don't you?' And then when she didn't answer, *'Don't* you?'

'Yes, I do!' she screamed at him. 'I bloody do!'

If he had not been so caught up enjoying his great victory, Hooper might have noted this as an historical moment, perhaps the last time he would hear this wild, free howl of the she-wolf. Things were so much muddier now and people hated to look foolish and out of date – even Sally must hate to be behind the times. Probably it had taken courage for her to release the old brave battle-cry. Hooper couldn't have cared less. 'Fine!' he cried exultantly. 'Well, you stick up for your side and I'll stick up for mine.'

'You prick, Hooper,' she breathed.

'You cunt, Stein.'

'Oh, Bill,' she wailed. 'I was at your wedding!'

'I forgive you.'

He hung up. Creighton had been listening with interest to his end of the call. 'Anything up?' he enquired politely.

'Just an old friend.'

'Oh, that's all right,' he nodded, and they got on with their work.

Hooper felt he could bear becoming a pariah. He felt quite defiant about it, particularly when he remembered that those old friends had not been such staunch supports in his own time of agony. And in any case, not everybody was completely hostile. One day he finally went to see how Amy Dunn was doing. She had just had the stitches taken out of her back, and she told him she was feeling all right now, just afraid to go out on the street. They talked about what had happened to her for a while and then, after they had fallen into a silence, she cleared her throat nervously and said, 'Look, I know I'm supposed to be taking sides on what's been happening, but I don't know . . . I'm not sure what side's what these days. I'm too confused.'

He was grateful for this much. 'We'll stay friends then. Shall we?'

'All right.'

She said something then that stayed in his mind after he had left her. 'You know, sitting here, I've been thinking – about friends and things. I don't know . . . I just don't feel the same about them any more. I haven't for a long time, I think.'

He wondered what had brought this on. 'But they've all come to see you, haven't they?'

'Oh, yes. Every one. You're the last . . . It's not their fault. It's me. It's how I feel.

Hooper watched her worriedly. This was not like Amy. Not at all. 'How do you feel?' he asked her.

'I don't know.' She thought for a moment. And then, in a low, rather thrilling voice, she murmured, 'I feel I'm in a state of emotional recession . . . '

Hooper bowed his head, impressed. When he looked up he saw that she was grinning at him slightly. 'I think I must have read that somewhere,' she confessed. 'That's all I do nowadays. Read. And think. All the same,' she went on, more seriously, 'it's true in a way: I don't feel I've got a lot to give away any more.'

24

He was mostly worried at this time about Emmy's response to what had happened, and how it would affect their uncertain new friendship. He had his answer one day when he invited her over to look at a flat he was interested in buying. It turned out she had met Cheryl Langford at women's conferences back in the 'Seventies and had no love for her. 'She was a patronising bitch!' Emmy fumed violently. He watched her uneasily. After so many months apart, he had forgotten how much anger she always seemed to have stored up inside her. 'She called me "the mighty atom" once. In front of *hundreds* of women . . . Look,' she assured him, 'it's not as if your friend ran off with the kid. The judge made a decision he'd make a better parent that she would. So that's the end of it as far as I'm concerned.'

'We wouldn't have done anything, but she told him she was taking Richard to Australia.'

'Well, she had no right to do that – '

'And I thought we were just going after a solicitor's letter,' he said in a quiet voice. Emmy didn't seem to hear him. 'You've got nothing to be ashamed of,' she said.

'Sally Stein thinks I have.'

'Oh, *Sally*!' laughed Emmy scornfully.

They moved around the flat. It looked good to him, saving the prevailing khaki and light-green wallpaper.

'How much do they want for it?'

'Twenty-six thousand.'

'That's good, isn't it?'

'It's not bad.'

She went and looked out of the living-room window. Across the road was a line of terraced houses identical to the one they were in, and like theirs mostly divided into flats. Not looking round, she said, 'One thing it seems to me – if you're getting a flat, it means you're not planning on ever coming back to me.'

He stayed by the door, not speaking. She turned and looked across the empty room. 'You never were serious, were you?' she said sadly.

'Yes, I was! Bloody serious . . . Look. Do you want me back? Do you think we could make a go of it?'

His words hung in the air like a challenge. She looked scared, and he knew undoubtedly he looked the same.

'Well . . . what if I said "yes"?'

'Go ahead. I'll do it,' he claimed, and waited with shrinking heart for her verdict.

'You've got your eyes closed!' she accused.

'Not at all.' He opened them as wide as he could. 'There. See? And I'm laughing!' A strangled croak emerged from his throat.

'You'd hate it if I said "yes".'

'Just try me.' Then, all at once, he gave up the pretence. 'We were pretty bad by the end. Weren't we?'

'We were awful,' she agreed gloomily.

He came and stood by her at the window. 'Look. Getting a flat . . . it doesn't mean that much. Any time we want to live together again, I'll just sell it.'

'And meantime?'

'Meantime, we'll bring up Christopher.'

'What if we have other people, meantime? . . . Either of us?'

'I don't know.' He stared out at the little houses over the way. He didn't know. 'I'll try not to make a fuss. If I can have a part of Christopher.'

'You do. You always will. You're his *father*.'

'But what if you start living with somebody?'

'I'll never do that again,' she vowed. 'The idea gives me asthma.'

They smiled at each other suddenly with great relief. And then she frowned. 'What's it all been about?' she sighed. 'We could have done this months ago, without all this fuss.'

'It wouldn't have been decent,' Hooper said virtuously. 'I have these deep feelings for you – '

'Only you can't stand to live with me,' she said angrily, and walked out of the room.

'Nor can you!' he called after her. 'With me.'

He found her sitting, head bowed, on the little flight of stairs that led from the hall up to the second bedroom.

'If you're not coming back,' she said, 'you can move the tea-chest out of my bedroom. I'm tired of storing your junk.'

He heard this reference to his unfinished *oeuvre* without protest.

'We've wasted such a lot of time,' she muttered.

He watched her with unmixed affection, now he knew he was out of danger. 'I want you to be happy,' he said. 'I feel such responsibility for you.'

'Oh, Bill, *why*?' she protested, but she couldn't help grinning in spite of her annoyance.

'Because I ruined you . . . Look what you were when I met you.'

'Oh for Christ's sake!'

'You were a *genius*, Em.'

'Rubbish! I was a little girl who was good at sums. I didn't want all that. I was a freak. I don't regret chucking it at all.' She jumped up energetically and struck an attitude. *'Non, je ne regrette rien!'* she sang, Piaf-style.

'Shirley Bassey to the life.'

She stuck her tongue out at him, and resumed her place on the stairs. 'Anyway,' she said, 'You were pretty much of a catch yourself back then.'

' "I could have had anybody at university",' he quoted at her, ' "and I took you".'

'I was lucky to get you . . . Editor of the paper – '

'Only for a term,' he reminded her. 'While Kenny had hepatitis.'

'National celebrity.'

'My slashing editorials,' he nodded, warming to her praise.

He couldn't remember much now about the content of those editorials, except that he had certainly overworked the phrase 'fascist scum'. They had caused quite a stir. The university authorities had finally closed the paper down, which had led in turn to protests and demonstrations that had embroiled the campus for weeks. 'National celebrity' was going too far, though the row had been given some coverage by Fleet Street, including a smudged photo in the *Daily Mail* of Hooper addressing a rally outside the student union building under a banner which read LBJ = HITLER = STEBBINGS. Stebbings was the university vice-chancellor, a working-class success, a staunch Labour man all his days. Hooper still had the cuttings on this somewhere.

In a while, his reminiscent smile faded, and he felt suddenly rather hollow and depressed. Emmy was still courageous, however.

'We were definitely the best couple on campus,' she declared.

'There wasn't a great deal of competition.'

'Even so . . . ' She held out her hand and he pulled her to her feet. They stood facing each other and, Hooper supposed, a certain look came into his eyes for she groaned suddenly.

'Oh, no! It's me running down the steps of the Tate, isn't it?'

'I can't help it. It was a great moment. The greatest in my life.'

She inclined her heads towards him. 'It's not hot any more, is it?' she said sombrely.

He touched it. It was stone-cold.

'Perhaps a faint glow,' he lied for her.

'Like hell!' she grumbled, pulling away from him. She looked at him bleakly. 'I don't care. I wouldn't go back to those days if you paid me.'

'You were just saying we were the best couple on campus.'

'I was humouring you.'

He watched her sorrowfully. 'There must be something you miss.'

'Nothing I care about,' she said toughly.

She walked out of the flat's front door, and after a moment he followed her. He knew that to some extent she had been posing just then, but he knew too she had spoken the essential truth about herself. It was not that she could not look back on many old things with affection. But she lived pretty squarely in the present. The past held no super-heated glamour for her. She was not wired up to it, as he often thought himself to be, like a poor, doomed laboratory animal forced to salivate or wag its tail on cue. He envied her for it.

All the same, as he locked the outer door of the flat, he felt the undercurrent of an old disappointment he had felt about her. He remembered that in the past, when they had lived together, he had sometimes thought that there was something large and vital missing from Emmy's composition. Sally Stein had once told her over dinner that she was completely lacking a 'poetic dimension' – which was good coming from Sally. Yet the accusation had stuck with Hooper, and he often turned it over in his mind, as he was doing now, and often too decided it had hit the mark, or close to it.

And yet, as he walked back alone to return the key to the estate agent, he found himself remembering too an evening when he had discovered Emmy in tears in the living-room of their flat. She had been sitting there, in the twilight, looking out at the May blossom that grew in profusion under their window. In the beauty of the flowers she had suddenly seen, as in sharp contrast, her own plight. Seen that life was passing without richness and was getting no better, that there was no radiance in her existence with him, no beauty and almost no life. It was nine months before he had actually broken up that existence by leaving home, and he had always thought it was an action done by himself alone and resisted by Emmy. But really he could see now that the marriage had been pronounced dead, finally and irrevocably over, on that evening when she had shown him how far away they were from the May blossom.

25

That night he slept badly and kept waking. Something was troubling him about his meeting with Emmy. It seemed to him – though in the night it did not present itself coherently at any one time – that a bargain had been struck between them to protect each other's rights over Christopher. In these patches of wakefulness, he feared that they might have constructed too an intricate trap for themselves, a kind of limbo, empty and seamless, in which they would drift through life, side by side but never touching, never having each other properly, never having anyone else properly . . .

Where's my chance to start again? he wondered fearfully.

And at another time, he thought: I shouldn't go back to the Common. I shouldn't cross the river again. I should go live in . . . America . . . or Paris . . . or Kentish Town . . . or anywhere else.

Around three o'clock he thought clearly of another relationship he had mangled.

It would have been better if she'd gone to Australia, he mourned. A clean break. For both of them it would have been better. For all of us. Oh Christ . . .

And for the children, he thought later.

He fell asleep at dawn and slept deeply for three more hours. When he woke again he did not remember that his sleep had ever been disturbed. After breakfast it occurred to him to ring up Roger Miles who he hadn't seen for a while. Roger had left for work already, but his mother said she'd tell him he'd called. In the late afternoon Roger rang Hooper at his office. He seemed pleased that they were in contact again. They fixed up a meeting for Friday, two days away.

26

He was waiting at his front-garden gate when Hooper drove up. He said he wanted to 'get away from the house', so they walked over to a new place that had opened up on the other side of the Common.

It was not a pub, or a wine bar, or a restaurant exactly, though it did serve food too – the nearest to it Hooper had seen before we the 'life-style bars' he had visited in the SoHo district of New York; and there were moments too when it reminded him of the modish brilliance of Leonard Scruby's office. Behind the long shimmering bar, skinny young men in designer jeans and tennis shirts or singlets moved lightly but purposefully about, shovelling ice into shakers, pouring out cocktails, crowning the brimming drinks with slices of orange and lime and pineapple, and little paper umbrellas and even – Hooper could hardly believe it when he first saw it – miniature Mars Bars. This, he read in the cocktail menu, was for a concoction called 'Big and Dusky'. Most of the drinks had more or less suggestive names: 'Virgin's Prayer', 'Hot Pants', 'Green Grope'. Hooper, after thought, ordered a 'Frigid Mama' – a mix of tequila, vodka, blue curaçao and soda water; Roger had a rum, gin and blackcurrant combination entitled 'Oh, My Cherry!'

After they had their first sips they looked at each other.

'Well, there's no alcohol in this,' Roger stated.

'There must be,' Hooper argued. 'We saw him put it in.'

But its presence was hardly detectable and at two pounds fifty a cocktail it seemed a bad bargain. Thereafter, they ordered American beers.

Neither of them was a practised drinker and after four or five Budweisers each they were both glowing exaltedly, laughing loudly at each other's jokes, tapping their feet and swaying the upper halves of their bodies to the beat of the anonymous but emphatic taped music that rumbled through the room, looking round eagerly at the Friday night crowd as the place filled up.

It was a young clientele, Hooper thought – he and Roger were nearly the oldest ones there. And it was a *clean* clientele, he saw. Many of the young men wore monogrammed tennis shirts like the boys behind the counter and crisp new jeans or pressed cotton slacks, and gleaming white trainer shoes. Their hair was cut in clean 'Thirties styles. There was certainly no hint of the beer-belly slovenliness of the pub-drinker here. No hint of the latter's drunkenness either, and having sampled a cocktail Hooper could see why. It was fine with him – he disliked inebriation in others.

'You'd probably have to spend fifty quid to get smashed here,' he told Roger. It seemed a perfectly straightforward statement and he said it five times but still Roger couldn't seem to grasp it.

At one point Hooper caught sight of a familiar face in a group that was seated in wicker chairs round a glass table on the other side of the room. He waved excitedly. It was

Tom Smallwood, one of the young people in Editorial at Overton's. Tom didn't seem to notice him though Hooper waved and waved. He would have gone over to the group except it seemed suddenly unbelievably risky to leave his bar-stool.

'I hope he's not spending all his money,' he said to Roger worriedly when he'd given up trying to attract young Tom's attention. 'I happen to know he's getting fired next week.'

'Good show!' cried Roger, who must have misunderstood him. 'Have another beer.'

'Well, just one,' said Hooper cautiously, for he was feeling a little peculiar. His waving seemed to have transferred itself to his stomach.

It was mysterious. One moment they weren't there, and then they were. Two German girls. Hedwig and Ursula. They were over here 'to study English'. Hedwig would like a 'Long, Slow Screw', Ursula picked a 'Martian's Crotch'.

'. . . Slow Screw, please, and a Martian's – ' It suddenly struck Hooper what he was saying and he began to heave with laughter. 'And a Martian's – ha! ha! ha! – a Martian's – ho! ho! – '

'And a Martian's Crotch,' snapped the boy behind the bar. 'What's so fucking funny?'

He marched off to mix the drinks. Hooper looked anxiously round for Roger. 'I think we forgot to tip him,' he whispered loudly.

But Roger was fully engaged with their new friends. They were, it emerged, great lovers of England. Hedwig professed herself particularly enamoured of the English sense of humour, though she didn't seem to find any of the jokes Hooper told very funny. In fact after the first couple of minutes neither of them paid him much attention at all. It was Roger who was the focus of all their interest. Hooper had not seen him in this role before and he was impressed. He made them laugh and he made them sigh and when he started talking modestly but eloquently about his work, his long, dedicated labours on behalf of the little children of Clapham's poor, he almost made them cry.

'I'm a marketing manager at Overton's,' Hooper said, but nobody was listening.

He recognised that it was not his night and he gave up the struggle. Sobriety seemed to be returning very fast anyway, and though he ordered and quickly drank down another Budweiser it made no difference. He felt cold and clear-headed and rather bitter, rather envious. Then he saw that this was quite wrong of him. Good Lord, he thought, Roger had a few happy times coming to him after all. He sat and listened to the others laugh and talk and compliment each other and wondered which one his friend would get off with. Hedwig or Ursula?

But then, after an hour of delivering uninterrupted charm and intelligence and cordiality, Roger changed absolutely, as if a switch had been thrown suddenly within him. He became silly, boastful, sexy in a crude, callow way. He became insulting. From somewhere – and Hooper's heart sank particularly to see this – he dredged up some sad old impersonations of Monty Python impersonations of the *Colditz Story* and began heiling the girls, shouting 'Jawohl, mein Kapitän!' to the bar-boy and 'Get stuffed, mein führer!' to Hooper when he tried to make him desist. The German girls were at first astonished, then angry, and then they grew extremely bored. Usula departed for the Ladies room and did not return. Hedwig sat on for a while, stonily watching Roger's antics through her cigarette smoke.

Roger became enormously, obnoxiously loving towards Hooper, embracing him over and over, and kissing him several times on his cheeks. 'This is my friend,' he called over his shoulder to Hedwig. 'Mein freund, ja? My best friend. Aren't you, Bill?'

Fuck you, thought Hooper coldly. You're not my best friend, not by a long chalk. But to Roger he just smiled in a sickly way as he tried to break out of his arms.

'That's right, Roger,' he said. 'Best friends.'

'You don't know what a freund he's been!' cried Roger, easily resisting Hooper's attempts to shake him off.

Hedwig stepped down from her bar-stool and reached to the counter for her packet of Marlboro and her lighter. 'I sink perhaps you are a pair of homosexuals,' she said indifferently.

This struck Roger as hugely funny. He would have fallen over if Hooper hadn't held him up.

'No, you're wrong!' he wheezed at last. 'It's my *wife* . . . My wife! *She's* the homosexual . . . Bill'll tell you.' He tightened his grip round Hooper's neck and Hooper gasped in pain. 'Bill knows all about it!' He looked round for the German girl. But Hedwig was no longer there.

'Let go of me, Roger . . . You're *hurting* me.'

'Am I, Bill? Am I really? What a shame!'

'Let *go*.'

'Glad to!' said Roger, releasing him suddenly with a smile.

Hooper afterwards couldn't remember much about the rest of the night. After closing-time released them from the life-style bar, he helped Roger across the Common to his home. It possibly took them five hours. First Roger wanted to share with him the fruits of a recent school project and this took a lot of time – about a Roman general called Asclepiodotus who in the year 296 AD had won a great victory over the native Britons on the land now taken up by the Common. Roger insisted in fighting several mock-engagements with Hooper to commemorate the battle. Hooper, whose neck was still burning from the effect of his companion's recent unprovoked assault, seized the opportunity to land several hard kicks and blows on Roger's body. Roger grunted in surprise and mild reproach each time they landed, but he didn't retaliate in kind. The blows he aimed at Hooper were gentle and slow in coming, and arrived with the force of soft slaps. After a while, Hooper grew ashamed of himself and stopped his serious attack. The two friends circled each other slowly thenceforth, delivering weightless cuffs at one another every now and then. Though Hooper couldn't help himself at one point stooping, grabbing up a clod of earth, and hurling it violently at Roger's head. Fortunately, it missed.

After the battle – and this took even longer – Roger insisted that neither of them should stir another step until they had both proved able to pronounce the general's name, quickly and correctly, three times in a row.

'Asclepiodotus, Asclepiodotus, Asclepiodotus,' said Hooper impatiently. 'Now come on, Roger – '

'All right,' Roger nodded. 'You're through. Now me . . . Aslepi-, Asclepio, Ascle-, As- . . . '

Very much later, when they were half-way across the Common, three youths loomed suddenly out of the shadows. In the faint lamplight their brutal faces gleamed with interest and anticipation. Hooper's first instinct was to flee, leaving Roger behind as bait to delay the pursuit. But, though inclined to panic easily, Hooper was not fundamentally a coward, and in the end, with the hopeless fortitude of an Ancient Briton facing the might of the Roman, he resolved to hold his ground. He saw that the moment of final confrontation in his great feud with Terry T and Danny T had come at last. He did not think he would survive it.

The most ferocious-looking of the youths opened his cracked and snarling lips. 'Hello, Mr Miles,' he said. 'D'you remember us?'

It was an emotional moment. Seven or eight years had gone by since these lads had sat in Roger's class and, in his present state, after the initial joyful greetings, their old teacher could not stop himself dropping a few tears at the cruel passing of time. And one of the boys too began to snuffle a bit. The others comforted him. 'It's all right, Dave,' they told him in tender, moving tones. 'It's OK . . . '

The boys had a couple of bottles of wine with them – common source, Hooper brooded cynically, of all these easy tears – and they insisted on sharing them with the men. Roger had several deep swallows and Hooper took a quick drink too for fear of seeming stand-offish. The boys and their teacher then sat down on the ground for a chat, and Hooper too, trying and failing not to think of dog-shit, eventually squatted down beside them.

In the thin lamplight he watched the others moodily. He could hardly hear them, he did not care very much what they were saying anyway. Looking around, there was nothing much else to see. Complete blackness began within a few feet, broken only by faint spots of light from the lamps further down the path. Hooper wished he was almost anywhere else but where he was. He considered leaving Roger to get home alone. But he couldn't do it. He felt responsible for the man – though for no reason that pressingly occurred to him. And he was deeply suspicious of these boys. They seemed very cordial and affectionate with their old teacher now. But they could so easily turn on him, Hooper reckoned. Steal the stupid drunk's money, beat him up. He had to stay and provide what protection he could. There was no help for it.

But still as he shifted on the cold ground his spirit rebelled against his being here, in such a place at such an hour – and with such companions! In this frame of mind, his thoughts turned sour and loftily despairing. I am not with the right people, Hooper lamented to himself.

And then: I never *am* with the right people.

And worst of all; I don't even know who the right people are any more.

It was not always thus, Hooper brooded.

For once he had believed himself surrounded by fine and lively minds. He had coveted no other circles, groups, cliques than his own. Not in the world. He had thought, without a doubt, that his own friends were the best, the very best, that they knew more, saw more, and could teach him more than any others. Even now, looking back, he would not say that he had been wrong to believe all this . . . But that was then. Now – and he wasn't at all sure exactly when it had happened – he knew that it wasn't so any more. He seemed to have lost most of his old friends lately, but . . . it didn't seem such a loss after all. He might miss them as pals; but the old excitement, challenge, discovery that he had found in their company, all that had gone long ago, that was not there to be missed. Though their words were still often bold and defiant, behind them he sensed they had all become about as dull, fearful, and at sea as he himself now usually felt.

At least . . . almost all. Staring into the darkness, Hooper could think of just two people in his acquaintance whose company still gave him the old barbed pleasure of discovery and a sense that they still met the world with the edge of a point of view instead of curling up before it in self-protection like everyone else. And neither of them, he realised heavily, was available to him. He would never get started with Mark Varda. That was clear. He had offended the barrister in some final, irredeemable way. Quite how he had done it was unclear to him, but he had done it, for sure. There was no hope there.

And the other – the other was Jane Powell. Whose progress through life, which had seemed to stutter and fail somewhat of late, appeared to have picked up new force. Hooper had lately heard through Emmy that Jane was very much in line, was almost certain, to be selected for a winnable parliamentary seat. She was busily engaged now in cleaning up her image. 'She's booted out all her fifteen-year-old friends,' Emmy had reported in catty reflex. 'And she looks wonderful,' she'd added sincerely. How much Hooper would have enjoyed in the old days settling down cosily with Janey one evening to talk over this new development. He would have shown understanding, of course, and admiration too, for Jane enjoyed being flattered as long as it was not laid on too thick. But he would have been able to tease her a little also, reminding her of her old fierce antipathy to any such conventional ambition as a parliamentary career. Remind her, in fact, of her Cuban period, his old Janey. They would have discussed seriously the dangers of co-optation. And Hooper, instancing but not insisting on his expert position as a figure in the publishing world, would have warned her of the certain hazing she would get from the numbskull sections of the press. They might have ended up, he mused happily, falling about laughing, plotting for her to deliver a maiden speech in the Commons of unparalleled obscenity. What an evening it would have been! Even though the winter wind, sweeping free across the Common, was making his teeth chatter violently, Hooper could not help grinning at the thought.

He soon stopped, for the wind blew even stronger and he had to shut his mouth for fear his tongue would freeze up. And even more chilling was his realisation that it would never happen, such an evening could not happen now. Some while back – and Hooper knew it was long before he had got caught up in Roger Miles's custody case – Jane Powell had taken a decision about him, had concluded that she could get along very well without him, without his understanding, flattery, teasing, warnings, jokes. It was all excess baggage to her now. In her severe regard, Hooper had dropped out of the list of those who counted.

It was a bleak thought for Hooper, even more so because he entirely agreed with her decision. He guessed that she had detected in him some final, incorrigible frivolity. And it was so. He could never deny it. Frivolity, thoughtlessness, childishness – they had guided all his behaviour for too long to seem an aberration. They had brought him to the great mess he had made of his life. Had delivered him to the sorrows and storms of the past few months. Had led him, inexorably, step by step, even to this ghastly, lowering, and incredibly uncomfortable experience he was enduring right now. From the chance to mingle with such fruitful, thrusting, and effective figures as Varda and Powell, he had been demoted, rightfully, to – he turned and looked at his present associates with utmost loathing and scorn – to the 2 a.m. company of a dim junior school teacher and three mindless hooligans.

They were all laughing at something that had just been said. The dim junior school teacher had his great head back and was guffawing happily up at the stars. The hooligans were sprawled about, choking and wheezing with mirth. They looked as if they were having a very good time. Watching them, Hooper rather wished he had heard the joke that had produced this outburst. He could have done with a laugh. And it looked a warmer way to pass the time than to sit, as he had been doing, moping and berating himself. He felt extremely left out of things. They seemed really such a merry bunch . . .

All at once, Hooper found himself appalled by the arrogance of his previous thoughts. To be thus contemptuous of Roger, who, in spite of his strange behaviour in the bar tonight, had been such a good friend and companion to him all these months. And to dismiss without a moment's hesitation these boys beside him. Without a single attempt to get to know, to even speak to any of them! And it occurred to him suddenly, as he watched the others laughing and shouting – they had finished one bottle now, they had moved on to the other – that he was, in fact, passing up a fine opportunity by his summary rejection. For all this time he had been watching Terry T and Danny T from afar, having thoughts about them, fears, suspicions, dread imaginings, like a white settler thirty years ago studying the restless Kikuyu from behind the barbed wire. And this was his chance to *talk* to one of them. Which he was throwing away in his foolish, élitist spasm. Hooper groaned inwardly at this new evidence of folly. Again he congratulated Varda and Powell for their very good sense in having nothing to do with him.

He wondered if it was too late to make amends. He stared fixedly at the youth nearest to him. The boy's head was shaven close to the skull. A long scar ran from his right ear to the corner of his mouth. Affixed to one nostril was what Hooper had first thought was snot, but now perceived to be an item of personal jewellery. What a sight! he grinned to himself. And then shook his head angrily. This was an old trick, he knew. To dismiss the young because of their appearance. Thus it had been in his own youth, with the long hair and everything. He had no excuse for not avoiding this trap . . . He tried again. Stared and stared at the boy. It came to him with a mild shock that it would take no biological freak at all for him to be parent to this large, savage-looking individual. He was probably about sixteen, Hooper was thirty-five – thirty-six, he corrected himself instantly. It was very possible then . . . though what the fact signified was not especially clear to him. Certainly it didn't seem to help much right now. He tried hard to think of something to say to the fellow. It would be, he thought, delightful after all this time of suspicion and distant dislike to find himself actually talking on level terms with one of these youngsters. There was Roger nattering easily away to them. Evidently it was not an impossible dream he was entertaining. Why, Hooper might even find that he could learn something from this boy. He might even – he swallowed excitedly at the though – have something to teach him. He stared and stared.

It was no good. Nothing occurred to Hooper to say. Nothing stirred in his brain, no matter how hard and long he watched the youth. He did not know whether it was his own deadness or the boy's impenetrability, but he just felt nothing. Except his customary feelings whenever he looked at someone of this age of fear and pity, tinged with boredom. Probably it was his own fault, he concluded at last. Almost certainly.

The boy, at length noticing Hooper's fixed stare, became restive and then uncertainly belligerent. 'What you looking at?' he demanded.

'Nothing,' said Hooper sadly, and looked away. A barrier had fallen forever, he might as well accept it. He was cut off from the country of youth for always.

Then, gloriously, it came to him that there was one avenue left to him. That he had a child and that the child was the way back. Looking now into the darkness, Hooper's spirits danced in gratitude at his good fortune. He was a father, and it meant that he was not after all just a prisoner prosaically within his own generation. Through Christopher he would experience all the old things once again. Yet they would be new too, he thought excitedly, for Christopher and his contemporaries would be new. He could see more or less the boy rising through school, perhaps college. But beyond that? Would they still have jobs, professions when Christopher's turn came round? At any rate, presumably, he would be bringing girls home on day. Or – Hooper hesitated, then loyal to the fading shade of his generation, added resolutely – or be bringing boys home. Or whatever. If the world should last, Hooper would have that intimacy once again with all that he had to leave behind him. If only the earth would last, and if only – Hooper prayed suddenly, fervently – it was girls that took Christopher's fancy, his father would have links into the future for as long as it would ever matter to him. Even though, Hooper mused in quiet wonder, he had crazily tried to throw all these opportunities away. But it was all right now. The pact he had made with Emmy – so sensible, so mature, was there hope for him yet? – guaranteed that through his child he still had this grasp on time. The thought was superb to Hooper, like a song starting up within him.

As he was thinking thus happily, the boy next to him thrust the half-empty wine bottle in his direction. Perhaps it was a peace-offering. Hooper accepted it gladly. 'Cheers!' he cried. And when he handed the bottle back, he smiled at the boy. My son, he thought. I have a son. 'And what's your name?' he asked kindly.

'None of your fucking business,' the youth pointed out, and from then on ignored him severely. Hooper was sad about this, but no longer despairing. For: I am a father, he told himself over and over. I have my little boy . . .

At some time or other, the youths finally got up and staggered off into the darkness, their fond, ragged goodbyes still reaching the men long after they had disappeared from sight. At some time, much later, Hooper was able to get Roger to his feet too and aimed towards his own side of the Common. At last, as the first flush of daylight was touching the rooftops, they arrived back at Roger's house. Roger wouldn't go indoors. 'I don't want to see my bloody parents,' he grunted.

'Well, what are you going to do?' Hooper demanded wearily. ''Cause I'm not hanging about any more.'

'I'm going to stay here,' said Roger. And he stepped on to his small front lawn. He sank to his knees. Then stretched out full-length on his belly.

Hooper looked down at him. There was dew on the grass, but it wasn't raining, and it had got less cold with the sunrise. He didn't see how Roger could come to much harm there for a few hours.

'All right,' he said. 'Goodbye.'

Roger muttered something, but as if in his sleep.

As he got into his car Hooper thought, That's *it*. I've done my duty now.

27

After a weekend of indecision, he finally decided to make an offer for the flat.

'Do you think twenty-six thousand is OK?' he asked Creighton Phillips on Monday morning. 'Two beds, central heating, small garden out back.'

'Sounds like a steal. Where is it?'

'Clapham.'

'Ah. In that case, try an offer.'

'How much?'

'50p!' twinkled Creighton, who commuted every day from Sevenoaks. 'But be prepared to go up to a quid.'

In the end, Hooper offered £25,250, which was accepted very fast. And since there was no one living in the flat and he had nothing to sell, the whole deal went through in five weeks. During all this time he did not visit Roger Miles. He bore him no grudge on account of their long night out. He could not, in fact, remember too much about it. Looking back, it seemed to him to have been quite a funny experience after all, though he had no wish to repeat it. He met Roger by chance out walking on the Common one day. Neither referred to their last meeting. Roger looked rather harassed, though he told Hooper again that everything was fine. Hooper told him they were going to be neighbours shortly and his friend smiled and asked where he was moving to.

'Just off Northside – the right side, I suppose Graham Greene would say.'

After that they did not seem to have much more to talk about. Just before they parted, Hooper gave him the number of the telephone that was in the flat and told him the day he planned to move in. The phone wouldn't be turned on till he was living there, but he urged Roger to give him a ring any time after that.

'And I'll come round and see you definitely before then.'

But he didn't. He had plenty of things to do, of course. The flat, first and foremost. And then a week at a publishing fair in Brussels. And after that he was kept very busy at the office completing the plans for the launch of Overton's World Cup one-off for next summer. There were not really too many opportunities to visit Roger. But the truth was that Hooper hardly thought of him either, and only once did he talk with anybody else about the things the two of them had gone through together.

This was with Creighton Phillips in the pub one Friday after work. After a couple of drinks Hooper found himself spilling out a stream of details about Roger, Cheryl, the case, the lawyers . . . At which point, for the first time, Creighton took a real interest.

'Varda?'

'Mark Varda.'

'I knew a Mark Varda. How old is he? 'Bout our age?'

'Suppose so,' nodded Hooper.

'Must be him. What's yours like?'

'Tall. Dark. Good-looking. Rich. How about yours?'

'Small. Fat. Smelly. Miserable.'

Hooper shook his head doubtfully. 'Doesn't sound like the same. He sails boats and things . . . Where was this you knew him?'

'Prep school in Dorset.'

He hadn't expected anything so conventional from Creighton, whose father had been an executive with ICI. The son had been educated exotically round the world. Lycée in Chad. Boarding schools in New Zealand, Hong Kong and South Africa. Creighton had finished up by taking a degree in marketing at the Wharton School of Business in Philadelphia. (He was actually much better qualified for Hooper's position than Hooper was. They dallied sometimes with the idea of swapping jobs without telling anyone. They were pretty sure their superiors would never notice.) And now a prep school in Dorset . . .

'It must be him,' Creighton argued. 'It's not a very common name.'

Hooper shook his head again, still unconvinced. 'Small and fat, you say?'

'And smelly. And believe me, to have a reputation for being smelly at that place, you really had to pong . . . We used to call him "Shit-bum".'

'Shit-bum?'

'Yes. It was a really super school, as you can tell. Unfortunately, the name was very apt . . . Poor little sod,' Creighton sighed. 'I think his parents took him away in the end, he got bullied so badly . . . Anyway, you might ask him. St Julian's Lower School. Near Weymouth.'

'I shouldn't think I'll be seeing him again,' Hooper said. 'In any case, he doesn't seem to like to talk to me much.'

'Actually,' said Creighton uneasily, 'perhaps you'd better keep quiet about if after all. As I recall we gave poor Shit-bum hell. There was talk of the police when he was taken away.' He drank his whisky gloomily. 'And I believe I led the pack,' he confessed at last.

28

One other major preoccupation kept Hooper from thinking about Roger Miles's affairs during this time. It started in Brussels, at the publishing fair. She was with the huge IPC delegation and they met at the disco party organised by her group on the second evening. Shouting at each other though the numbing racket from the sound system, they discovered that they were staying at the same hotel. After that evening they were staying in the same room.

It had been many months since Hooper had gone to bed with an attractive woman, or any woman, and as he prepared to make love to Mary Hall for the first time he was suffering from severe stage fright. When they were naked, the sight of the unimpressive erection he had thus far managed did nothing to reassure him. In these situations he was always cursed by his long-held doubts about the acceptability of the male, body and soul, in woman's eyes. He was keenly regretting having gone along with Mary's gently-offered suggestion that they spend the night together. A humiliating failure in this arena was just what he didn't need, he though, when he had so recently established a fragile stability in his life.

But then, suddenly, even as he was fearfully glancing down at his wilting penis, she leaned over and in one unbroken movement scooped up a drop of moisture from its tip with her forefinger and conveyed it to her mouth. 'Ah – nectar!' she sighed, with an enthusiasm which even he could not deny was genuine. And after that it was more than all right.

When they got back to London he saw a great deal of Mary for a time. She lived in N16, near Clissold Park, in one room at the top of a house. It was a dark house in a dark street, but she had made her room very bright and pleasing with light shades of paint on the walls and potted plants and flowers all around. She spent a lot of time in that room, though she was one of the busiest people he had known. She worked for IPC two or three days a week on a freelance basis, on fairly humdrum design and paste-up work. (She had wangled the trip to Brussels only when one of the staff workers had dropped out at the last moment.) Her true work was her own painting which she pursued with an unselfconscious commitment that Hooper found constantly intriguing. For she seemed to have no professional instincts at all, had no desire to make a show, or a name, or money or anything that he could really understand. She just liked to paint – and this was strange to him for everyone else he knew was either furiously and self-importantly dedicated to their careers or, like him, resigned to coasting along at something they couldn't really care much about but which gave them the means to pursue an adequate social or family life. But she did her work at IPC solely so she could spend the rest of her time painting, without thought of reward, it seemed. He tried to probe this sometimes, wondering if it was timidity and fear of failure that kept her from striving for recognition. It was, after all, what he guessed had held him back from ever achieving anything. And laziness. And other things . . . But it didn't seem to apply to her. She just seemed happy working on her small canvasses in the patchy light that fell from her windows, and when she'd finished, hanging them for a time on her walls and then stacking them away or giving them to her friends. Though she would take money for them too. Hooper paid her twenty pounds for one.

She painted mostly interiors, rooms or hallways or

stairs, and if she ever took her vision out of doors, it was still to something that was enclosed, behind walls and fences – a garden, or a yard, or a swimming-pool. Many of her subjects were set in Los Angeles where she had spent three years before coming back to live in London six months ago. He liked her work – though he was too unsure of his judgment in these things to do much more than indicate approval. When he tried to be specific he always came out with something magazineish and deflating, as when he remarked of her California paintings that it was 'a pity Hockney got there first'. The look of surprise she gave him when he said that made him ashamed. It seemed never to have occurred to her that her choice of subjects or her pleasure in what she did could be affected by what anyone else had done. She was a competitor in no race, and for her the whole withering critical jargon – 'influence', 'in the school of ', 'major figures', 'minor figures', 'seminal', 'derivative' – did not exist. He concluded that she was *hors de combat* in the best possible way – though sometimes too he wondered if she was kidding herself.

Mary was twenty-five, ten years and more younger than Hooper and his friends and almost all the women he had slept with before. He could not help wondering if the very great ease and lack of complication that he experienced with her, in and out of bed, had something to do with her comparative youth. His relations with the women of his own age had most usually resembled the manoeuvrings of grand armies as the two sides negotiated the terms and, after elaborate parleys, established the conditions on which they might, tentatively and suspiciously, lie down and come together. Of course, his judgment may have been affected by the fact that since he had met Emmy he had never before gone to bed with anyone he cared much about. But still it felt like a real difference, and he was often tempted to think surreptitiously that it was because with Mary they both 'knew their places' and there was little risk of confusion and of deadly scrapping for the same small piece of ground.

Naturally, a cynic – and Hooper prided himself on being that – might suspect that he took such pleasure in knowing 'his place' because it happened to be on top, and it was true that he had a constant impression of being served when he was with her. Afterwards, his characteristic image from that time was of himself lounging in or on her bed, eating something she had just made for him and chattering away about his own preoccupations while she listened silently, all the while painting away at her easel, except when she got up to pour him another cup of tea. There *was* something of the geisha about Mary, an effect heightened by her neat, black, shiny hair and by her eyes which had a slight perceptible slant. She also used a lot of make-up, in contrast to the women of his age, contributing further to the Noh effect. Christopher met her once and thereafter called her 'the made-up lady'.

Yet Hooper was sure that he did not feel at the time that she was somehow humbled because she gave so much to him. It was not extorted from her, she offered it with untroubled enthusiasm. And he thought, in fact, that much of this service was because he always happened to be a guest in her home. He could not take her to the hotel and he was still not yet in his flat. They used to talk a lot about the famous meals that he would serve her when at last he had his own place.

In bed too he was served, greatly. Most of all in bed. She was a skilful lover, seeming always delighted to have him with her, committed to his pleasure and, with hands and mouth and admiring exclamations, paying a special flattering interest to his cock. This was so outside Hooper's experience that for a long time he thought it was all make-believe. But eventually, even he succumbed to her constancy and began to entertain the revolutionary notion that a woman could be unambiguously attracted to a man's body. His body. She came to her orgasm very easily too, either with him or, if she needed, reaching down while he was still inside her and giving herself a few quick rubs – and he praised heaven in those moments that this particular burden had been lifted from him after so long.

Sometimes the guilty thought attacked him that he should be doing more for her, but it was soon washed away in all the tender insistence of her giving. And he *did* pleasure her too, in his way. She liked most of all to listen to the long and sinuous and ultra-lewd stories that he whispered to her in the darkness as they made love. His mighty member. Her shivering twat. The legions of men who waited hopelessly all over London and in Los Angeles too, a tall forest of waving cocks, desperate to fill her famously tight and molten cunt with white, burning . . . Sometimes he thought that all the creativity that he had once hoped would result in books and plays and poems was pouring out into Mary's ear. But it was all right. He had found his lover's erogenous zone, and from her gasps and murmurs and sometimes screams of excitement as she listened he knew that never had woman before been taken on such rude and ecstatic journeys. Never round Clissold Park anyway.

Hooper found too – and at first it disconcerted him – that these tales of throbbing members roused him very much also. Though he had often expressed sincere solidarity with his gay brothers, in fact – and he swore it was only a result of schoolboy conditioning – he had always rather shrunk from the contemplation of such acts. But with Mary all things became possible and alluring. She was a lovely woman for him. And a lovely boy. She spurred him on all the time to yet denser and more lascivious imaginings. The bed they shared was crowded with a host of extravagant and indefatigable companions, licking, sucking, browsing, thrusting . . . Yet he knew, as he lay shuddering against her, that they were all Mary in the end. And afterwards he was very glad to hold on to her single form, hold her tightly in simple gratitude.

They were happy together. From this time, Hooper remembered waking up many mornings in her bright room. She liked to sleep with open windows and the air was always cold in his nostrils. But he was snug in bed with Mary, her warm buttocks pressed against him, his hand around her warm breast; and if he waited for a while, he knew she would get up and light the fire and make them both a pot of tea.

Towards the end of this period, however, he began to see less of her, and he was not sure exactly why. There were some problems, particularly the awful bulk of London and its impacted traffic that he had to fight through whenever he went to see her or came away. But this should have been a trivial drawback. He was aware that, much as he appreciated the serenity, the *niceness* of their co-existence, it seemed sometimes to be rather flat round Mary's home. Except when they made love, he often felt that something was missing, without being exactly sure what it might be.

The most depressing thought for him, when he worried about this situation, was that he was so accustomed, his emotions were so in thrall to the difficult, driven, ambivalent, and astonishing women of his own generation that he had lost the ability to be satisfied for long with someone as straightforwardly good for him as was Mary Hall.

29

The phone was turned on the morning he at last moved into the flat. Half an hour later he had his first caller.

'How's it going?'

'Oh, fine, thanks,' Hooper told Roger. 'I've started painting the front room. The wallpaper's holding up. Weird pattern underneath – but it's OK . . . ' He was aware that he was chattering on somewhat. 'They're putting up the venetian blinds next week . . . The beds came today.'

'Beds?'

'One for me. One for Christopher.'

'Oh, right.'

Hooper opened his mouth to say more, and then found there was nothing else he could think of to say. He stared at the patch of wall he had just been painting. There were a few bubbles showing up under the paint. He hoped it wouldn't get too bad.

'I just thought you'd like to know,' Roger said then, in a particularly casual voice, 'that the final hearing's next week.'

All at once Hooper realised how much he had been hoping not to have this information, how much he'd really been hoping that Roger wouldn't even get in touch. Lately he'd been pampered by Mary, and by Emmy too in her way, into thinking of himself as almost a good man. He didn't want these sad, old troubles to rise up again to show him any other possibilities.

'I just though you'd like to know,' Roger said again.

There was no escape. Hooper saw he had to see it through to the end.

'I'll come along,' he said sadly. 'When is it?'

'You don't have to.'

'When is it, Roger?'

'Eleven o'clock, Tuesday morning.'

From where he was standing, he could see his front windows. They were pretty grubby. He would have to wash them down before they put the venetian blinds up. The idea for them had come from Leonard Scruby's office. 'I suppose it's a foregone conclusion,' he said into the phone.

'I think so . . . We've seen the welfare officer's report.'

Eleven o'clock, Tuesday morning hung over him dourly for the rest of the week. Fortunately, he had taken a few days of holiday to work on the flat, and the steady, fruitful monotony of painting got him through it without too much pain. Ladders and rollers and paint-trays and white spirit and the breezy drone of Capital Radio – it was like being in a trance after a while, a hard-working trance, and he slept exhausted every night on his brand-new double bed. The glossy decorating manuals that he consulted told him that sombre shades were all the rage now but, inspired by Mary's example, he chose only light colours – magnolia in the living-room and his bedroom, white in the kitchen, and light-blue with cream trim in Christopher's room. It was a treat to watch the flat come alive.

Meanwhile there was Tuesday. He walked over to the court-house that morning, telling himself with every step that it was for the last time. Once again he went into court in the guise of a solicitor's clerk. The proceedings were, if anything, even less dramatic than before, and there were parts that had been cut or were being played by understudies. Roger was there and so were Judge Kirby-Smith, Mark Varda and Jane Powell. But Cheryl hadn't shown up, and nor had Scruby, who had sent a young man from his office who spent his time looking covertly through an issue of *Vintage Car*.

Both sides had received copies of the social-welfare officer's report, but Kirby-Smith asked her to read them out in court anyway. Both reports were positive – only Roger's was slightly the more so. His house was clean and spacious, the boy had his own room and a garden to play in too. Roger's job was giving him plenty of time to be with his son, and the presence of the grandparents was an additional benefit. Cheryl's new home too was clean and spacious, though not as spacious as her husband's, and there was no garden. It was clear that the two women shared a bedroom, and in conversation with the officer there had been no attempt to disguise the nature of the relationship between them.

Pathetically, the little boy had been included in the welfare officer's investigation. Under questioning,

Richard had confessed that he liked his mother very much, and he liked his father too.

The atmosphere in the room was lumpy and flat, as they all waited for the inevitable. Hooper watched the judge as he scratched away at his notes. The deep-blue drape behind Kirby-Smith's chair gave him an idea for a colour for the street-door of the house his flat was in. Royal-blue would present a nicely dignified exterior to the world. He supposed though he would have to check it with the people who lived upstairs as they shared the same front door.

'I think it's in the best interests of the child that we let matters stand as they are,' stated Judge Kirby-Smith after a couple of preliminary remarks. The young man next to Hooper looked up from his magazine and made a note on the cover of the manila folder that rested on the table before him. Jane Powell stood up.

'Your Honour, arrangements for access have been worked out to the satisfaction of both parties.'

'Yes . . . ' The judge picked up a piece of paper and inspected it. 'I see there is no provision that the boy may not be taken to the mother's present home.'

'Your Honour – ' Mark Varda was on his feet. 'We have no objection to the happening.'

'You may not, Mr Varda,' remarked the judge smartly, 'but I do . . . I shall make such a provision.' His Honour scribbled away, while the two lawyers exchanged looks. Mark Varda shook his head apologetically. The judge set his pen aside at last. 'If the mother should ever leave her present address, she is entitled to come back and request that it be lifted.'

'Your Honour, I'm obliged,' muttered Jane Powell.

30

It was all over. Varda passed in the court-room to talk with Janey. Roger and Hooper and the man from Scruby's office went out into the lobby. Roger spoke for a while with the young man, and then came and joined Hooper.

'Well . . .'

'Yes . . .'

Which seemed to exhaust what they had to say to one another, and after a while Roger went off to look for a lavatory. He had not come back when Varda emerged from the court-room. After hesitating for a moment, he walked over to join Hooper. They looked each other over. Nearby a barrister, in gown and wig, was talking to a boy with a Mohican haircut and a tattooed skull, presumably his client. They seemed to be having an argument.

'Congratulations,' Hooper mumbled at last to Varda.

He saw then that the barrister was staring at him with interested eyes. 'Tell me something,' Varda said. 'Just to satisfy my curiosity. Is there anything similar to this in your own life?'

'I'm sorry?'

'Well . . . a broken marriage? Separation? A child you're afraid of losing?'

'. . . I suppose so.'

'Yes,' nodded Mark Varda with great satisfaction. 'There so often is in these cases. The crony in the background. Working out their own anger vicariously. How interesting,' he mused. 'I've only known it to happen with women clients up to now. But apparently there's no difference between the sexes. As in so many things, I shouldn't wonder . . . What would you say?'

Hooper said nothing. Varda surveyed him cheerfully. 'Well, I hope you got what you wanted out of this,' he said. 'And perhaps you'll be coming to me on your own behalf one of these days.'

'I won't,' Hooper snapped. 'My wife is blameless.'

'How unfortunate!' the other laughed. 'For both of us. Although, of course, he went on laughing, 'we abolished the concept of blame in these matters years ago!'

He had had enough of Mark Varda. Had enough of his clever remarks and his bumptiousness and his contempt and his ludicrous fees. 'Tell me, Varda. Something I'd like to ask you . . . ' Oh, I can play rough, too, thought Hooper, if I want. 'Does the name "Shit-bum" mean anything to you?'

But he was worth his six hundred pounds a day after all. He stared at Hooper for a moment. And then, 'What an extraordinary thing to say!' he murmured. And he turned resolutely away, as if the other did not and never had existed, to greet his client who was returning across the lobby, leaving Hooper forever uncertain whether the look of sheer terror he thought he had seen for a moment in the barrister's dark eyes had been really there or was just the product of his hopeful imagination.

As Roger neared them, a strange thing happened. The young man nearby with the Mohican haircut suddenly drove his fist into his barrister's stomach. His face comical with surprise and pain, the barrister sank to his knees. There was a moment's shocked silence in the lobby. Then Varda rushed forward to the aid of his colleague. There was a general surge towards the youthful assailant – police, lawyers, witnesses, defendants, all lunging to get their hands on him. Roger disappeared from view behind the mélée.

Still standing where he had been speaking to Mark Varda, Hooper realised suddenly that the last thing in the world he wanted now was the company of his friend. He took advantage of the uproar to slip out of the building through the revolving doors.

He walked briskly down to the Junction and then set off up Lavender Hill. 'You've got to put everything behind you now,' he was saying to himself, over and over, as he marched along. And, 'What can't be cured, must be endured.' And, 'No use crying over spilt milk.' And any other cliché that occurred to him that might help him over this last small hurdle. As soon as he got back into his own home, and back to painting, decorating, improving, he was sure it would be all right. 'Let the dead bury the dead,' he murmured to himself, wondering if it was too strong for the occasion. There was only half a mile or so to go now to safety.

But then, standing waiting at a zebra crossing, he looked back towards the Junction and saw to his discomfort that Roger Miles was hurrying after him.

Hooper ducked into Altenburg Gardens and ran towards the Common. After a few strides, he heard footsteps closing in on him from behind. He ran faster, but the footsteps still gained on him. In a little while Roger was running along beside him. They didn't speak. They were like two joggers out on a companionable run. And then, suddenly, it turned into a race. They were going flat out. Hooper strained his every muscle, grabbing great lungfuls of air, driving his arms and legs along – but it was no use. Roger easily pulled away from him. Soon he was ten yards ahead.

In this manner, one behind the other, they broke out of Altenburg Gardens and on to the Northside. It was the morning of a one-day rail strike and traffic was piled up even thicker than usual. The fumes hung yellowly in the still grey air and got deep into their lungs. By the time they reached the grass and then the low asphalt mountain, Hooper was coughing and heaving, somewhat from the exertion, but mostly from the foul stuff in his throat.

'Goddamn this filthy, horrible place,' he gasped, as he stagged to a halt on top of the little hill. 'I hate this place!'

'Yes,' said Roger, turning back towards him. He was breathing hard, but not choking like Hooper.

'The hell with it,' raged Hooper. 'I wish they'd build on it!'

'All right,' said Roger.

Hooper stared angrily at the other man. 'What was that

general? That Roman general who fought here. What was his name?'

'Asclepiodotus?'

'Yes . . . well, the hell with him too.'

Roger looked out from the top of the hill towards the Southside, his side of the Common.

'Incidentally,' he said. 'This hill. You were nearly right.'

'What?' said Hooper, who had almost got his breath back.

'It is a bomb-shelter. But for the last war. There's nothing down here now.'

After a moment, Hooper asked. 'How do you know?'

'Rang the council. They told me.'

'Ah, you,' breathed Hooper at last. 'You believe anything you're told, don't you? Any stupid thing.'

Roger laughed.

'You make me so fucking angry,' Hooper scowled.

'I can see that.'

They stared at each other. Hooper was the first to look away. 'I feel like hell,' he said. And as Roger watched him. 'It's true. I hated Emmy and I thought I'd lost Christopher. And I put it all on to you.'

Roger still watched. Hooper hung his head. 'You would never have done all this if it hadn't been for me . . . Would you?'

'Yes, I would,' Roger said.

Hooper stared at him, affronted. 'You bloody wouldn't.'

'*You* only wanted us to get a solicitor's letter.'

'Absolutely untrue!' snapped Hooper.

And then he cut his hand through the air as if to decapitate the pointless quarrel.

'I played a part in it, didn't I? You can't deny that.'

'All right. You played a part.'

'I pushed you. And I didn't do it for you . . . Maybe you and Cheryl could have worked it out if I'd left you alone. I didn't think. I never even asked you what the bloody problem was between you, why she left, anything. I didn't think about anyone else but me. From the start . . . I just wanted to hit out.' He looked wretchedly up at Roger.

Roger smiled. 'I know that.'

'What?'

'Well, I'm not an *idiot*.'

After a moment, Roger said, 'Why don't you come back home with me?'

Hooper shook his head. 'If you don't mind, I think I'll just – '

'Yes,' nodded Roger. 'I think you should.'

He turned and walked down the hill and started across the grass towards the Southside. After twenty yards he looked back at Hooper. 'Come on,' he called.

Hooper, at last, began slowly to follow him.

'Come on, Bill,' Roger encouraged him again.

31

Richard was sitting in the kitchen crayoning on a sketching-pad. Cheryl was beside him. She looked up as the two men came into the room. She smiled tentatively at her husband.

'How is he?' Roger asked her, going to touch his son's forehead. 'He's got a bit of a cold,' he explained to Hooper. 'Couldn't go to playgroup.'

'He's all right,' said Cheryl Langford, putting her arm round the little boy's shoulders. 'Hardly a sneeze.'

Roger began to describe for her the morning's proceedings in court. She watched him solemnly all the while, but did not show much emotion, not even when he told her about the judge's new provision that her son could not visit her in her home.

'Of course that won't make any difference,' he said to

her, and she nodded, still watching him with the same grave regard.

Hooper stood in a corner of the room. He kept his eyes lowered mostly, but from time to time he cast brief glances at the woman. He was confused by what was happening here. He supposed he would get an explanation in time. Now he concentrated secretly on Cheryl. She seemed to him very different from the last time he had seen her in this room when she had stood boldly in the doorway firing questions at him. And yet he could not say exactly why she was different. Perhaps she was a little thinner in the face, the skin more tightly drawn, but that, he was sure, was not it. Something had changed – but he could not tell what. Whatever it was though, it made him sad to see it. He wondered if Roger had noticed it too.

Once she turned her head and looked in his direction. He could see no expression at all in her eyes. They did not seem to focus on him. She's pretending I'm not here, he thought. It was certainly convincing, her pretence.

When Roger had finished speaking, Cheryl stood up and put on her coat. 'I must go,' she said.

Roger watched her for a moment. Then, 'Thanks love,' he said. He turned away and picked up the electric kettle. 'I'll bring him over tomorrow night.'

'Right.' She kissed Richard, then headed for the door. ''Bye!' she waved at her husband and son.

'Cheryl!'

She whipped round. Stared anxiously at her husband. Roger smiled at her 'You've forgotten your bag.'

'Oh . . . thanks.' She came to retrieve it. 'I'll forget my own head one day.' She smiled brightly at no one in particular. And then, ''Bye!' she said again to Roger and Richard. And was gone.

Richard went upstairs to fetch some more crayons from his room. Roger stood at the sink filling the kettle. He plugged it in, then looked at Hooper.

'Her friend came to see me,' he said. 'About three weeks ago . . . She was worred about Cheryl. She wasn't eating and . . . ' He shrugged. 'Other things.'

He turned away to empty the coffee-pot. Hooper groped his way towards a chair.

'So I went to see her. And we had a talk . . . we had several talks. I told her all I wanted was to share Richard, not take him away from her . . . That's all I *ever* wanted,' Roger said passionately, as if there was an argument about it.

The kettle boiled. He switched it off. Hooper watched him.

'I just want to be his father while he's little, while he's young. And she saw, she understood . . . And that's what we're going to do. Share him. He'll stay with me sometimes, and with her sometimes. That's what he wants and what we want. That's what we'll do.'

Hooper shook his head. He felt horrified that he had to smash this dream. 'But you *can't*,' he explained. 'You've won custody. And the judge made an order Richard couldn't go to her house. It's against the law!'

'Oh, the *law*,' scoffed Roger grimly. 'Custody! If they don't know what we're doing, what can they do about it? And who's going to tell them? Are you?'

After a while, Hooper tried to sort this out. 'But why did you have to go through today, then? Why couldn't you just tell the judge that you'd worked it out between you?'

'That's what we thought we'd do,' Roger nodded. 'But when we told Jane Powell she said: on no account. After all the things I'd said against Cheryl, if I went to the judge and said it's OK after all, her being gay and everything – it's the old problem. He might have turned against both of us and have had Richard taken into care. So we had to go through the whole thing.'

'Did Varda know?'

For the first time Roger smiled. 'Didn't seem worth telling him.'

Hooper thought it over. After all, he couldn't really see any major flaws in this scheme. 'But what about Australia?'

'I think Cheryl's changed her mind,' Roger said, in a neutral tone. 'Apparently Australia is out . . . I gather her friend is going by herself now,' he added.

Richard came back into the room with his crayons at that moment and started again on his pictures. He worked swiftly – great, elaborate creations, sunbursts and rainbows and rocket-ships and green men with two heads and orange women with none. Roger bent over the sketch-pad with him and at his son's direction printed a title at the bottom of each work. One of them, Richard announced, was to be called, 'The Spanish Conquer the Universe'.

'The what?'

'The Spanish Conquer the Universe,' the child repeated firmly. Roger looked up at Hooper and shrugged helplessly. Then he bent over the pad again and wrote as his little boy had directed.

32

He stayed at Roger's house most of the rest of the day. And it was like old times, they talked and drank coffee and around five Roger made high tea for the three of them. Hooper felt good all day. The guilty weight he had been carrying around for so long had fallen away from him. He told himself that it had all worked out, the circle had been completed, balance was back in the world. Sometimes that little phrase of Richard's passed through his mind. 'The Spanish Conquer the Universe.' Hooper relished it. It seemed to him to express that notion of victory against all the odds that he and Roger had achieved. They had come through their time of trouble. Like heroes now, they could rest on their laurels, in the knowledge of a triumph well-deserved and a fair peace at the end of it.

At one point Roger told him how glad he was to be on his own in the house once more. 'It's really strange living with your parents again,' he said.

'I can't imagine it,' said Hooper.

'It got bloody tense,' Roger admitted.

And late in the afternoon Hooper told Roger about something that had happened to him months ago, before he had met him. It had been, he thought, the most terrible event of his life and he had not been able to speak of it to anyone before, not Emmy, not any of his old friends, no one. It was just after he had found out that Emmy had a lover and in the first hours of his discovery that in his folly and thoughtlessness he might have given up his right of fatherhood. Emmy had wanted to go away for the weekend – and she didn't want to take Christopher with her. Clearly it was to be a holiday with her lover, though Hooper did not ask her, dared not then for his sanity even think of it. He had no place of his own to take Christopher, so he had driven down to some friends' cottage in Sussex. They only had one double bed spare for him and Christopher, so when the adults had finished talking that night – which was early for he was miserable company then – he had gone upstairs and climbed into bed beside his sleeping son.

Some time in the night Hooper had woken up sweating in terror – for he had seen with unbearable clarity that in his sleep he had wrapped his fingers round the little boy's throat and strangled him.

Christopher lay there, his face peaceful in the moonlight. Of course he was quite all right. Of course it had been a dream. But Hooper could not sleep any more that night. When he came to something like his senses, he gave himself explanations for what he had dreamed. He saw that he had turned his rage, his urge to murder, against Christopher because it was he who all innocently was causing him the greatest pain. It was the loss of him that Hooper dreaded above all things. It was not his boy he wanted to kill – but the fear that hung over him that his boy was lost to him.

So in this fashion he had tried to calm himself, and in

some degree he had succeeded. But he did not try to sleep any more that night. He would not while he shared a bed with Christopher. He believed he had seen how the mad might perform. And in his mind he could see, over and over, his own sleeping form and the hands moving forward without conscious volition to throttle the life out of the little boy who slept trustingly at his side. He stayed awake all that night for fear that if he slept he might kill his son.

'Maybe all this,' said Hooper – and by that he meant all that had happened to the two of them and all the people: Cheryl, and Emmy and Varda and Scruby and the Steins and Judge Kirby-Smith and Janey Powell . . . 'Maybe it means that I don't ever have to dream that dream again.'

'Then it's been worth it,' Roger said.

'Yes,' said Hooper.

But for some reason he still did not feel entirely content. There was something, he thought, that was still left unsaid. Something about Christopher. He didn't know what; and it puzzled him, just as it had puzzled him to watch Cheryl and not know how she'd changed.

It was time at last to go. Only one piece of business was left unfinished.

'When do you think you'll get the bills for all this?'

Roger looked up and smiled. 'I've alrady got one from Scruby.'

'Is it big?'

'Colossal!'

'I want to pay some of it.'

Roger shook his head. 'You've got a mortgage now.'

'I want to do it. I said I would.'

'No,' said Roger firmly. 'I'll manage.'

Roger walked him to the garden gate. A light rain was falling, the sky was turning towards evening. Hooper did not know what to say. He felt such affection for Roger and pleasure that it all seemed to have worked out for him. At the same time he thought they would probably not be seeing each other much any more. He knew Roger better now, would never again make the mistake of thinking of him as a 'plodder' or as the 'willing ox'. On the contrary, he thought Roger was quite a formidable man, quite dangerous in a secretive way. That was the problem, perhaps. Hooper knew himself to be drawn to more touching, vulnerable men. Like Creighton. Or Sam Stein. Except when he was in deep trouble, Roger lacked pathos – and Hooper, though not approving of himself for this, knew he neded that in another. He and Roger were like two passengers on a hijacked plane, thrown together for a while by the perils they had shared. But now it was all over, the scare had subsided, the terrorists were under lock and key, and they were back in their own lives again. Perhaps they would have a reunion dinner once in a while to talk over the old adventures . . .

Yet he wanted to convey the tenderness he felt just now – and he could not. And it seemed Roger was in the same predicament, for as they stood at the gate they could not for a long time get beyond a sort of boyish patting of each other's arms and shoulders, accompanied by gruff mutterings of 'Well, you know . . . ' and 'Take care . . . ' and 'listen, I'm really glad . . . '

But Hooper at last looked up squarely into his friend's face. 'It's worked out,' he said thankfully. 'Hasn't it? For everyone. And we did the right thing.' He waited for what seemed a long time to hear Roger agree with him. He wanted badly to hear that. And when Roger still did not respond: 'At least,' Hooper faltered, 'we did *something*.'

'Oh, yes,' Roger said. 'I think we jerked her lead all right.'

Hooper was several yards down the road when he turned and walked back to Roger Miles who was still standing at his garden gate.

'Why did you have to say that?' he said miserably. 'I wish you hadn't.'

'I know,' said Roger. In his hair and on his clothes raindrops were sparkling in the light from a street-lamp.

He looked up past Hooper to where the sky grew black over the Common. 'I wouldn't have said it – ' His eyes too were shimmering under the rain and the lamplight, as if they were filmed over with tears. 'Except it's true.'

She was not special any more. Hooper worked it out on his way home. She had been made ordinary. That was the difference with Cheryl Langford now.

33

More than anything, it was the crisis over the Falkland Islands – blowing suddenly into life a few weeks after Hooper's last visit to court – that eased his path back into the fold with his old friends.

Under the pressure of large events, even Sally Stein relented towards him – in fact, a couple of weeks after the crisis began, when the British task force was well on its way to the South Atlantic, she rang up to ask him to come over to her house. It was the first time she had spoken to him since their great row months before. The cause was Sam who, it appeared, was showing disturbing signs of belligerent patriotism.

'He's just gone,' she said. 'He's just regressed.'

She was trying clearly to keep her sense of humour, but Hooper had the feeling she wouldn't mind screaming either. He had the feeling too there had been bitter fighting lately in the Stein home. 'He's like when I found him,' Sally joked in a dry, unhappy way. 'When he had a horrible plastic bust of Churchill in his room. And a framed letter from Iain MacLeod . . . Oh, *please* come and talk to him, Bill,' she said urgently.

Sam had installed himself in a small back room at the top of the house. When Hooper pushed open the door, he found him sitting slouched in a battered armchair, frowning, staring at nothing. There were piles of newspapers and magazines around his feet, and two radios close at hand, and a portable television set. On one wall was a large map of the Atlantic Ocean. Sam had stuck pins in it to show the dispositions of the opposing forces. Red for the British. Yellow for Argentina.

'Is this the War Room?' smiled Hooper, putting his faith in humour.

'Shut up and get out,' snapped Sam Stein.

Hooper, smile fading, held his ground. 'Now, Sam – '

'I know what you're going to say and I don't want to hear it.' Sam got up and furiously paced about his little cell.

'*I* don't know what I'm going to say,' Hooper protested, advancing a couple of steps. 'But you've got everybody worried, Sam – '

'All I said,' Sam Stein fumed, 'was I thought for once Thatcher was doing the right thing. And my God did the roof fall in!'

They had had a long talk that afternoon, during which at one point Sam had said, 'You don't know, Bill . . . I've wanted so long to cheer for England. I've had such an ache to do that.' Sam had always claimed exultantly that his Jewishness spared him from the general contagion of belonging to the English nation, but in a way Hooper was not surprised to hear of this new direction. He recognised what he was beginning to see as a rule of life – the more fiercely someone expressed an opinion the more likely it was they were trying to drown out the siren songs that beckoned them towards the opposing camp. He thought of poory Cathy Tremayne who had tried to go out of life giggling, and of Tony Herring who had crossed from bombs to the Buddha. He thought of himself who had once argued for feminism against women.

He had no good news to tell Sally that day. But during the following week a truce was at last agreed between the couple. Sally conceded that the Argentinian military shouldn't have seized the islands; Sam admitted that the whole thing should never have happened in the first place, it was all the fault of Whitehall muddle. This settlement was largely the work of Kenny Herbert who sat and argued with Sam for nearly a whole night until he yielded. But Hooper was given credit for trying. As the crisis worsened and grew savage and bloody, the friends stopped taking positions and a mood of anxious despair settled on them. In this climate Hooper's misdeeds seemed unimportant, ancient history. They were forgotten or forgiven by almost all his old friends. Only Saint Jane Powell still refused to have anything to do with him.

One day in the heart of the war Hooper went out walking with Mary Hall. He had to tell her that he did not think they should see each other any more. Wanting to find the kindest way to explain it, a case for treatment probably, clinical, a hollow man now, incapable of caring for another, it was best that he be alone so that he could no longer do harm to anyone. He did not like saying these things about himself, particularly because he feared they might be true. And they didn't seem to help Mary very much. She cried, and she begged him to reconsider. He went through his reasons again. His inadequacy, his unworthiness, his sickness.

'I've got nothing to give you,' he urged her.

'But you *do*. You *have* . . . And I don't care anyway!'

Hooper wanted very much to concentrate on what was happening between them. He found it difficult. For he had gone the way of Sam Stein in one respect – he now hated being out of reach of a radio or television. The news bulletins obsessed him. There were terrible stories in them. Dogfights in the sky above the grey Atlantic. Deadly submarines prowling deep within it. Every night a gaunt looming man with a voice like an undertaker's appeared on the evening news to announce fresh disasters. An English ship had been blown apart the day before by a missile fired from forty miles away. The day before that an Argentine ship had gone down and hundreds of men had died . . .

'Oh, well,' sighed Mary at last. 'I guess these things just have their natural life, don't they?' It sounded like something she had been taught to say, in London or Los Angeles.

Hooper looked out on the alien sward of Clissold Park. There had been rain and the ground was spongy underfoot. He supposed that for many people this was an exceedingly pleasant spot, and there were features that recommended it – there was a little zoo, for instance, and a river. But it was not for him.

'I'm sorry,' he said for the twentieth time. He looked then at Mary. Remembering how good she had been to him, he thought he must be a great fool to let go of her. And he had done it. She seemed at last to have accepted his arguments. She was cheering up a little, he thought. The worst was over for her. For himself, he felt suddenly very cold and alone. She touched his arm. 'Never mind,' she said, kindly. 'It's nobody's fault.' They turned and began to walk slowly back to the exit.

When he listened to the news now he felt riven with a hundred emotions. He felt scared, elated, ashamed, sometimes he wanted to cry and sometimes to run out into the street and boast. Sometimes he saw Jack Hawkins on the bridge and sometimes it was only Terry T and Danny T on the rampage as usual . . . He glanced surreptitiously at his watch. There was a radio in his car. He truly wanted to give Mary every consideration on this, their last time together. At the same time, he had a strong, undiluted wish that they could wind this up before the early evening news.

'I used to think sometimes,' she said suddenly, 'it would have been nice to have had a baby with you. And it might have made a difference.'

'Oh, my God!' Hooper cried out, appalled. And then was shot through with remorse at the sight of her wounded face. He stopped walking. Took her hands in his. 'No. Mary. Really . . . ' There was a smear of mascara down one of her cheeks from when she had been crying. It irritated him suddenly to see it. Entirely too much make-up . . . Then he felt more remorseful than ever. He squeezed her hands. 'Don't think about it,' he said urgently. 'It would have been awful. Fatherhood . . . I can't – ' He couldn't. He was uncertain whether he was about to reveal himself to her, or only to make things up.

'Christopher . . . ' He shook his head. 'He broke us up,' he told her. 'Emmy and me – we could have made it if we hadn't had him. We'd have got past the bad times. We'd have looked after each other always . . . He finished us. He grabbed all the kindness and we had nothing left. He took it all . . . '

He looked past her into the park. Spring was bravely present here, breath of new life everywhere. He recoiled from it. Now she stroked his hand as if to comfort him. He felt so sorry about everything, and wished he could make it better. Most of all he wished right now he was back on his own side of the river.

'I didn't leave home because of Emmy,' he said, feeling as he spoke the words as if a fissure was opening in his heart. 'I left because of Christopher.'

It wasn't true. It surely wasn't. He went over his words many times in the days that followed until he had convinced himself of this. They were only a tactic to stop Mary from having needless regrets. He hoped they had worked. He never found out, for he did not see her again. The weeks passed. The strange war ended as suddenly as it had begun, and seemed set to become ancient history in its turn. Hooper and his friends tried mostly to forget it had ever happened – except that he had two long conversations with Sam Stein about their baffling reactions to the conflict while it was on. Their conclusion was that they remained baffled, thought it had been good to talk it over.

At one time during the summer, feeling very lonely, and angry with himself for doing it, he had rung Mary's flat several times but got no answer. He tried then to reach her through her employers, but was told that she no longer worked there. They could not exactly say where she was now, though there was a rumour in the office that she had gone to live in Germany.

Hooper dug in. He spent most of his free time making improvements to the flat and the back garden. He had a couple of small dinner parties and his friends were complimentary about the things he had done to his home. In the back garden, he tore down the old low rickety fence. He bought a new one, eight feet tall, with trellis-work along the top. As he was putting it up, he noticed his back-neighbour frowning bleakly down at him from an upstairs window. These were tiny gardens. The new fence was too high for them. He was probably cutting off light from his neighbour's kitchen window. However, the man never came to challenge him, and Hooper was not to be put off by sullen frowns. He decided he needed his high ramparts. He planted some climbing roses along the base of the fence. They didn't reach very high this first summer, but he had hopes for the years to come.

Though he lived now so close to the Common, Hooper seldom went out to it. He spent his time in his back-yard. He bought a deck-chair and sat out in the sun most evenings and weekends. He saw Emmy quite often at the times they passed the care of their child between them. It still amazed him that they lived apart. He dreamed about her sometimes, dreamed that they were still together. And he always woke up happy from these dreams. Yet when he saw her he was never tempted to suggest that they try again. Common sense forbade it. It seemed to him now, that all those years they had lived together, though they had bred such enmity between them, had also meant that, by proximity and starting so young, the two of them had ended up almost sharing the same bloodstream, as it were, supporting life on the same breathing system. To have divided at this point in their lives had been like submitting to a perilous operation. Hooper was still appalled to think how blithely he had invited it. Yet to knit the systems together again – and he did not know how else Emmy and he could share life together – would be to undergo surgery as jarring and dangerous as that which had parted them. And now, lacking ignorance, Hooper could not imagine volunteering for it. Only some huge, overriding impetus could push them towards that, he thought. And the only thing he could imagine of that nature would be some threat or disaster concerning Christopher. That was something too horrifying even to contemplate.

They were best off apart. In one area Hooper was certain of this. He took almost perfect pleasure now in the company of his child, and he was able to do this, he knew, because he saw him for strictly limited periods. In those times he could give himself completely to Christopher. And when they were over, his time was all his own. It was an experience of personal freedom that he had not had when they all three lived as a family, and which he knew had become precious to him. Above all there was no more endless squabbling with Emmy over whose turn it was to keep the child occupied. Their separate responsibilities were all set out now, clear and defined, with no room for grudges and misunderstandings.

As far as Hooper could tell – and he watched the little boy anxiously for contrary signs – Christopher had adapted to the situation very well. He seemed quite proud of having two homes and to be equally happy in either of them. Hooper had strong fears that the events of his childhood would surface unhappily in Christopher in ten, twenty, thirty years' time – but that, he conceded, he could not hope to control, and it would be pointless to stew in guilt over something that might not occur. Pointless too, out of guilt, to deny the advantages in what had happened. All in all, he came to believe that though it was a rotten situation, it had its compensations. Paul Mosby had called it thus so many months ago. Hooper had thought that his friend was attempting a feeble joke. Now he saw it had been kind of Paul to try and offer him this insight. He would like to thank him for it, though the other had probably forgotten their chat by now. Certainly

Paul's good intentions had been foredoomed. Hooper accepted that he was not a man who could take advantage of short cuts. Everything had to be proved to him in the living of it. Everything, over and over.

The rest of life more or less passed him by in this time. There was a sudden enormous crisis at work. Overton's was no longer profitable. The company had made huge losses, was deep in the red. There was a threat to close down most of its operations. Massive redundancies loomed. People gathered in fearful knots in the corridors, arguing, protesting. People burst out weeping at their desks; and all over the building the phones rang and rang unanswered. Creighton Phillips for one was beside himself with worry. Hooper basically sleep-walked through this period, earning himself thereby a reputation for fortitude and unflappability in the face of disaster. Particularly the younger people seemed to find him a rock of calm strength while all around were losing their heads. To his surprise, he became a sort of counsellor and cheerer-up to many of them. New sources of finance for the company appeared, and the immediate crisis passed. In its wake, to defend the interests of the employees better, a staff association was formed, which certain levels of management were entitled to join. To his even greater surprise, Hooper was invited by a deputation of his younger colleagues to run for president of the association. He declined to stand, pleading family and personal reasons.

In fact he was far too busy in his deck-chair to consider public office at this time. He had so much to think about. Errors to consider, idiocies, misunderstandings, false ideas. His old friend Amy Dunn sometimes came to sit with him. Hooper felt very kindly towards her, remembering how she had not turned away from him during the custody fight. She seemed in much better spirits than when she had been convalescing from the knife attack. ('Are you out of the emotional recession yet?' he asked her the first time she came over. 'Not quite,' she said carefully. 'But close to it.') He was surprised to discover that she who he had known for so long – cheerful, smiling, sentimental Amy – could display a very sharp and aggressive perception of life and people. She was much quicker than him. He would remember for a long time with embarrassment the day he had revealed to her – it was the product of a week's hard thinking – his theory that some of his difficulty in separating from Emmy was due to his reluctance to say farewell to his own youth. The look Amy gave him, almost one of pity, showed that this was very far from being a surprise to her.

Hooper had sunk back deep into his deck-chair. 'You know,' he'd said at last. 'I'm beginning to think that everybody else has been to some sort of school that I've not ever heard of. Why am I so bloody slow?'

'No, no,' she had assured him, in kindness. 'It's hard to see things about yourself. If it was somebody else, you'd have got it right away.'

But he continued to think that her mind worked much faster and more clearly than his – though that, he acknowledged, on his recent performance was no great compliment. He started then, before he had a chance to get himself confused or side-tracked, to talk things over with her from the beginning. He talked about Cheryl Langford with her one evening. Something which still bothered him, and, in fact, really frightened him was that she, who had been so strong, so tough, had after all toppled over like a pile of loose bricks when he and Roger had stood up to her.

'Was that all it was?' he lamented. 'Was she only strong because no one had ever challenged her before?' And he knew he was not just thinking of Cheryl when he mourned this possibility.

Amy leaned forward and stared at him. 'Cheryl was never strong,' she said.

Hooper gaped at her. 'What?'

'Never strong . . . She's really a very timid person.'

Hooper laughed out loud. He described to her the first time he had seen Cheryl – her boldness, and vigour, the challenges she threw out with every word and gesture.

'All a pose,' said Amy.

'Come *on*! What about the things she used to write? She wanted to kill people! She had – '

'Pure theatre.'

' – murder in her heart.'

'That may be so,' said Amy. 'Still it's true what I say . . . Look,' she insisted, as Hooper continued to look disbelieving. 'I *know* Cheryl. I've known her on and off since school. She gets anxiety attacks, fainting spells, the works. Her confidence goes so she poses away like mad and that works for a while and then she capsizes all over again . . . She's not *strong*. She was never strong. Not like Jane is. Or Emmy. Or Alice Carew. Or – ' She hesitated. Then tilted up her chin proudly. 'Or *me* . . . Believe me,' she finished. 'All you and Roger knocked over was a façade.'

When she had gone, and for many days after, Hooper puzzled over this conversation. Cheryl the timid instead of Cheryl the strong? It was a hard one to swallow, it seemed to run so much against the evidence. Yet he trusted Amy and it would be a relief in some respects to see these things through her eyes, not least because he had put so much into his admiration of his female friends and their hard-won strength and independence. It was certainly frightening to think that all that depended on his own agreement never to bunch up his fists and sock them hard between the eyes. It would be better to think of that as just a piece of presumption, a fantasy of power and vengeance. Yes, he would prefer to move Cheryl into a separate category of the not-so-strong. Yet there remained the fact, undeniable, that at one time she had been prepared to carry her child off far away, in despite of its father's desires and happiness. That was hardly the behaviour of a timid or weak person. Or was it? Hooper worried and worried at the problem and never quite cracked it.

The summer wore on. Hooper took to rising very early. He was in the deck-chair most mornings not long after dawn. It was lovely out there then. Already warm, and so silent it was as if no one else in the whole city was awake. In that peace, stretched out in his chair, he disputed earnestly within himself other notions, probably erroneous, that he had been clinging to. Particularly a set of attitudes which Amy on one visit had dismissed as 'Hooper's potted history of womankind'. As she'd described it, he saw things like a graph. A storm of female rage ten, fifteen years ago, and the line gradually but steadily dropping ever since.

'Listen,' she'd said. 'There are *plenty* of angry women around today. Me, for one!' she'd added cheerfully.

She brought him articles to read. Suggested programmes for him to watch. He pored over the evidence. He conceded that she had a point. There were protesting women everywhere today, visible and infuriated . . . And he had been perfectly well aware of this, of course. As he was aware of many things without actually taking them into account.

'All the same,' he said to Amy when she came round again, 'there *is* a difference between then and now. I'm sure there is.'

'Well, all right,' she nodded. And then, not without a certain pride. 'We were pioneers back then. We were like nothing that had gone before. And things are about issues mostly now. Back then we were – ' She stopped. And then laughed tenderly. 'We were just radiant about ourselves!'

He watched his old friend's lively face with pleasure and affection. From long habit he could not help noticing that there were some new lines on it, near the eyes, on the forehead. And the skin at her throat seemed rather loose. But these things interested him now, he believed, not because he still sought revenge; but because they reminded him of how long the two of them had been friends. And these were not flaws that Amy was displaying, in any case – they were badges of experience. A pioneer face, indeed! . . . He hoped very hard that this was truly how he felt. 'Also,' Amy resumed more seriously, 'things were entirely new for you too back then. You have to take that into account.'

'No, it's more than just that,' Hooper said slowly. 'I look at Emmy, say. Or look at you. Then at someone like Mary. It's not the same.'

'It's just different people, Bill. You can't make up a theory about it.'

He shook his head, unconvinced. She watched him. Then shrugged. 'I never knew Mary. How old is she?'

'Twenty-five, twenty-six.'

'Well, I know lots of women younger than that who're full of rage. There's a bunch of them living next door to me. Eighteen-year-old furies. Sixteen-year-old . . . '

'Are they really tough?'

'Well, they think they are,' she chucked. Then, 'I'd take you round to meet them – '

'That might be interesting.'

' – only they don't allow men inside their house.'

Hooper thought for a long time, staring at his high fence. 'I really know all this,' he said at last. 'It was just safer for me to think it all belonged to the past.'

She nodded. 'I can see that.' They sat for a while more in silence. 'You should get out of this garden, Bill,' she said at length, rather sadly.

He shook his head. 'I'm best off here,' he said. 'For the time being.' He believed he was. It was time to be solitary. No more of playing the villain or the fool or the spectator. He had jumped through enough hoops for the present. Even to talk with Amy was perhaps a luxury too rich. Enough. He should shut up now and think. Let the world go on without him. Particularly the world of women. He doubted he would be missed.

Autumn came at last in a sudden burst of bitter weather. But then there was a long spell of fine days and Hooper moved back out into his garden. Amy met a man at a party, an American journalist who was based, oddly enough, in Hamburg. There was a whirlwind romance. She proposed to leave everything and go to live with him. Almost all her friends were excited for her and enthusiastic about this development. Hooper counselled caution.

'Oh, *Bill,'* she protested. 'I'm ready for it now. I really am. And what have I got to lose?'

'Sanity?' he offered. 'Health? Life itself?'

She went off to Germany anyway. Thenceforth, he was almost entirely on his own. The cold weather returned. Hooper carefully stored his deck-chair away in the old air-raid shelter that served as a garden shed. He lingered then for a long time near his tall fence. In its newness it still gleamed garishly yellow, the wood rough and raw. But the winter winds and rain would mellow it, Hooper knew. It would be a different story when he came out to re-claim his garden in the spring. So too with his row of climbing roses. He had cut them back severely when the last blooms had dropped. They were only stunted sticks now, bare and prickly. But next year there would be roses everywhere, all the way up to the tops of the trellis.

He had much to be thankful for, he told himself. Sanity. Health. Life itself . . . And his child, good memories, good friends too, if he did not try their patience overmuch. The past didn't have to be lived through again, and the future was always concealed. Really it would be obscene not to confess that he was a fortunate man. He was alone now, would probably be for a long time to come. But what of that? he thought defiantly. He could endure that, he could take care of it. No problem. He remembered suddenly a ribald little song he had learned at school long ago. It was, he thought, about the only useful thing he could remember just now from all those years of school, exams, O-levels, A-levels, university, all that apparatus of study and aspiration that had led him at last to being a sort of recluse in his back garden and the Mr Chips of Overton's Publishing plc:

Last night
I lay in bed and pulled my pud;
It did me good,
I knew it would.

He raised his face to the iron sky and began lustily singing his song out loud. It crossed his mind that the uproar might be distressing his neighbours. He often thought that behind his high fence he was not just out of sight, but out of hearing, out of notice of all other people. That was an illusion, he knew – but really he was past caring:

First, I gave it a short stroke
And tickled the crown.
Then, I gave it a long stroke
Right up and down.

And how did it end?

People say that sexual intercourse
Is really very grand,
But speaking for myself
I'd rather hold it in my hand.

The winter my be fierce, Hooper grinned bravely, but I've got my central heating!

He waited beside the fence, his smile gradually fading. Next year, he whispered, next year . . . The cold and the silence began to get him down. After a while, he went indoors.

Bel Mooney
The Anderson Question

Bel Mooney was born and brought up in Liverpool. As a philosophy student at London University, she met her future husband, the broadcaster Jonathan Dimbleby. They now live near Bath with their son and daughter. THE WINDSURF BOY, her first novel, reached the *Sunday Times* bestseller list. Bel Mooney has worked as a journalist for a wide variety of publications and has appeared regularly on television and radio. She is now a regular columnist on the *Sunday Times*, and reviews fiction for *Cosmopolitan*.

'A novelist of perceptive strength . . . Bel Mooney plots an authentic, compelling detective story of the soul' COMPANY

Eleanor Anderson's comfortable and well-ordered life is completely shattered when her husband David, the dependable and much respected village doctor, disappears. A few days later he is found dead, apparently the victim of a heart attack, and speculation is stilled as family, friends and patients alike feel a kind of relief at knowing the worst.

But genuine grief at their bereavement gives way to angry bewilderment when a post-mortem reveals that the man they thought they knew so well, the man they all depended on, had taken his own life, for no obvious reason. And Eleanor discovers, in the uneasy company of her ungracious son, that all she had assumed and lived by has been false . . .

'She writes sensitively of a close village life, and tenderly of the anguish and soul-searching in his wife that Anderson's death provokes . . . it marks a real step forward in Bel Mooney's development as a remarkably good novelist' Susan Hill, GOOD HOUSEKEEPING

'Beautifully written, compassionate . . . extremely moving . . . one of the best novels I have read for a long time' BOOKS AND BOOKMEN

Piers Paul Read
A Married Man

'A moving and important book' John Mortimer, SUNDAY TIMES

'Eminently readable . . . a novel which is both subtle and powerful. The theme is discontent. John Strickland, a successful, middle-aged barrister, suddenly and overwhelmingly decides to change his life. He becomes a Labour MP, he stumbles into adultery and for the first time violence enters his life . . .' John Braine, SUNDAY TELEGRAPH

'Excellent . . . totally honest, totally absorbing and says many things which are worth saying' Auberon Waugh, EVENING STANDARD

By the author of the highly acclaimed novels *Game In Heaven with Tussy Marx*, *The Upstart* and *Polonaise*, and two striking non-fiction books, *Alive!* and *The Train Robbers*. *A Married Man* has been dramatized as a LWT production for Channel Four, starring Antony Hopkins.

Grace Ingoldby
Across the Water

Marking the debut of a remarkable new writer, ACROSS THE WATER is a novel about its characters – a family tragedy set in Co. Fermanagh during the summer drought of 1976. It is about two brothers – Desmond and Boyle Hamilton – who were sent 'across the water' to England to be educated. Desmond escaped from his Northern Irish roots, married an English girl and has become a trendy playwright in London. Boyle, now 40, still lives with his 'Dada' in the dilapidated Georgian family house, isolated in his own world behind huge wrought iron gates . . . Boyle is eccentric, close to madness, and he has maintained a friendship bordering on love with a 17-year-old Catholic youth suspected of complicity in the murder of their neighbour.

This murder is investigated by an English army officer who – as it turns out – was at school with Desmond and Boyle when they were 'across the water' Desmond's wife Aimee arrives to spend the summer – she's bored, conventional, middle-class and very English – and she drifts into an affair with the Englishman. Desmond arrives to make a pretentious film about Irish Celtic twilight and the ancient tradition of a stone which sits on an island in the lake . . . the island where Boyle's disturbed mind will finally crack and where the inevitable tragedy will take place . . .

'A first novel of rare authority, steeped in menace' DAILY TELEGRAPH

'A strong, confident and original debut . . . a gripping account of people in whom violence erupts' COSMOPOLITAN

'A strongly imagined and accomplished first novel . . . a horrible family tragedy played out by people exhausted in the heat and made threadbare by old, unresolved conflicts' THE GUARDIAN

'Accomplished and sure in its own right . . . you feel compelled to read on to the horrifying, beautifully described end' Susan Hill, GOOD HOUSEKEEPING

'The wit is accurate and very funny; trenchant, but never dismissive.'
Colin Greenland, NEW STATESMAN